GReads

Surfacing

Surfacing

KRISTIN HALBROOK

This is a work of fiction. All of the characters, organizations, and events portrayed in this novel are either products of the author's imagination or are used fictiously.

SURFACING

Copyright © 2014 by Kristin Halbrook

All rights reserved.

A Three Pixie Press Book

ISBN 978-0-9885859-6-6 (hardcover)
ISBN 978-0-9885859-7-3 (ebook)

For Suzie

1

My mother always claimed Tuesdays were the best days. No matter how bizarre and time-sucking her schedule as a pediatric oncologist was, she always, always had Tuesdays off. Like it was her spirit day, her Sabbath. It was the one day a week I really saw her, growing up. Until she left, and then I never saw her at all.

I suppose I've picked up her love of the day, hating horrible Monday for all the soul-sucking tasking and catch-up required that first day of the week, and feeling rather uninspired by that antsy "is the week almost over yet?" mood that falls into place right around Wednesday. On Tuesday, things feel fresh and clean and energizing. Promising.

I pulled my leather jacket on with a secret smile, and then checked my teeth in the bathroom mirror, making sure there was no spinach between them from my omelet this morning. I smoothed down my blonde hair, pulled a section over my shoulder and grabbed my messenger bag and my Chem textbook. Across the room, Chelsea Mathis' bed was as untidy as always. I was surprised not to have heard her come in last night, after I'd left the Theta Xi pool party early and she'd waved me off, saying she'd catch a safe ride back. But it was par for the course for me to sleep through her getting up and out the door before anyone else. She liked to hit the pool before classes. I liked keeping as healthy as the next person, but sleep was basically my favorite thing. Chelsea, on the other hand, was a force of nature.

My feet were light on the stairs to the first floor of the house. In the sitting room, Candace White and Madison Taylor gossiped at the speed of light about the party last night and picked at their breakfast scones until they were more crumbles than anything else.

"Good morning, ladies," I said.

"Hi Katie," they said in unison.

"I love your skirt," Madison added.

I twirled. "You're the sweetest. Your hair looks really pretty today." She flipped her soft brown curls off her shoulder with a smile. "I'm off. Have a great day of classes."

The morning sun warmed the sidewalk outside the beautiful contemporary Spanish Delta Gamma house. Bruins up and down the row headed to campus for class. Heather Loose and Janice Garcia from Chi O down the block ran to catch up with me.

"Are the numbers in yet?" Heather asked.

"Not yet. But when they are, you'd better warm up your scooping muscles." Delta Gamma and Chi Omega had made a bet that whoever raised the most money at yesterday's kickoff to the Spring Carnival for Charity—a preliminary event to warm-up for the bigger Carnival fundraisers—got a sundae party courtesy of the loser. Chi O may have had more girls, but I knew we had more style. And money. As President—and best friend of Chelsea Mathis, the Philanthropy Chair—I knew I'd find out for sure first in my house.

"Dream on, bitch," Janice said good-naturedly.

"How's Hector?" Last night at the Theta Xi party, Janice and her on-again-off-again boyfriend of two years, Hector, looked like they were in an on-again phase. Making out so hard in the crowded pool I thought they would drown. If not in the pool, then in each other's spit. But I'd left early, so didn't see if they were off by the end of the night.

"Delish." She licked her lips and grinned.

"Did you see if Chelsea got her ride okay?"

"Sorry, Katie, I wasn't paying attention. But I'm sure she was fine. You know Chelsea."

Yeah, I knew Chelsea. Better than anyone else. And she always had both feet on the ground, seeming effortlessly put together when the rest of us were scrambling to *look* like we had it all under control.

"I'll just see her in class," I said.

When we reached Young Hall, Heather and Janice waved bye and continued on toward the Court of Sciences while I entered and headed upstairs to my chemistry lab. Most of my class was already inside, but Professor Griffin hated phones on in class so I paused with my shoulder against the wall and checked my messages before turning it off. I frowned. Nothing this morning from Chelsea. Or Damon.

"What are you doing?" a voice hissed behind me.

I spun around. "Hey!" Damon grabbed me in a bear hug, his paws traveling down my back to cup around my ass. When I pulled away, I noticed his eyes were still red. I wondered what time he'd stopped drinking last night. "What are you doing over here?"

Damon shrugged his muscular shoulders and tossed his dark hair out of his face with a flip of his head. His t-shirt was rolled up to reveal round, tan biceps.

I had to hide a smile. I didn't want to look too eager to see my boyfriend, even if the morning sun was hitting his tanned body like he was some kind of Greek God. He hooked his arm around my waist and gave me his wide grin. I ran my palms over his arms. Rock hard. A delicious, warm tingle ran up the back of my legs.

"Thought I'd come wish my little woman a good day."

I faked a shocked grimace and twirled out of his embrace. He did that sometimes, those totally sexist comments that delayed my smile a tenth of a second. I was pretty sure he did it on purpose, knowing his teasing would get a rise out of me. "Little woman my ass. I'm no Rosalind Franklin."

Damon blinked. It was a good thing his lashes were so dark and pretty or else his puzzled expression would have pissed me off. "Who?"

"Just a brilliant lady scientist who was robbed by the guys. As usual."

"Oh please. You girls act like you have it so rough, but you know guys bend over backwards to get some."

He pulled me back against his chest and tucked his fingers under my chin to tip it up for a kiss. There was a part of me that didn't want him to do that. That wanted him to let me decide to kiss him on my own. But another part of me liked how much he wanted me. And it's not like I wouldn't have kissed him. Damon was hot, popular and wealthy, and we made the perfect couple.

"Do you athletes do anything but play sports and sit around and daydream about sex?"

"Well, sometimes we *watch* sports and daydream about sex at the same time. Or play beer pong and daydream about sex. Or take a shower and . . ."

"Stop right there! I don't need to know more than that."

Damon laughed and pressed his hips against mine. "Come over after classes?"

"I'm studying all afternoon. You know, that thing you do when you open books and complete assignments?"

"Is that what we're here for? I thought it was to daydream about—"

I spun away from him again, throwing a last flirty look over my shoulder. "I'll be late for class. Call you later."

#

I twirled my pencil and checked the clock, focusing on what students in the class were wearing, what they were doing, who they were looking at. Anything to keep my mind from drifting off into clouded corners of thought. Almost forty minutes had passed and Chelsea hadn't shown up. I furrowed my brow.

Across the room, Terrell Watson and Murphy Klein flicked wadded balls of paper at each other like they were still in high school, not seniors in college. Science nerds. I stifled the giggle that bubbled up in my throat. Chelsea always called us science nerds. We were the only science majors in DG and that had made us instant BFFs three years ago when we first met. If we could take a class together, we did. We helped each other with everything, but were highly competitive, too. Her grade in this class was slightly higher than mine right now, but I was owning Physical Biochem.

Someday, she and I would take science academia by storm, with our brains and our fashionable redesigned lab coats. Because we were girls who wanted to have it all.

I jotted down some lab notes, then looked up to find Professor Griffin glance anxiously at Chelsea's usual spot next to me. He and Chelsea had always been kind of flirty. He caught my eye when he noticed me looking at him and looked away quickly. I frowned. It wasn't like Chels to miss class, and she had been gone from our room before I was awake this morning. Where was she? I pulled my phone into my lap, sneaking glances at Griffin, and turned it on with one hand while writing more notes with my other hand. Once fired up, I sent her a text full of question marks.

Professor Griffin cleared his throat and I thought I was done for. But his planned words were cut off by the slightly muffled sound of a ringtone behind us. The whole class paused and looked up, turning towards the tall cupboards at the back of the room.

I knew that ringtone. That bell sound that made Chelsea stop whatever she was doing to see who was thinking about her at that moment.

But loads of people would have had the same ringtone, surely. My thumb moved lightly over my phone screen. A heavy feeling built in the pit of my stomach. I looked down. Typed *Hey woman!* and sent it to Chelsea. My ears pricked up.

The ringtone came from the cupboards again.

Had Chelsea come late last night to study and left her phone behind? That would explain why she was missing classes. She always relied on my alarm to get us up in the morning, but if she'd stayed over somewhere else and forgot her phone, she'd probably overslept.

So why hadn't she come back here to look for it?

The class was still puzzling over the sound in the closet, but no one moved toward it. Instead, one person after another looked at me, realizing I held my own phone in my palm. I set the phone on the top of my table and rose. Locked eyes with Professor Griffin, whose face was a mixture of curiosity and apprehension. Thought about telling him that I'd check out the sound. Laugh about how Chelsea was always losing something. But I couldn't get my throat to work properly. My swallow was thick.

The screeching of the legs of my chair against the linoleum floor made me wince. I stood and crossed the few steps to the back of the room, the silence in the room causing a vacuum in my ears, like the retreat of an ocean wave. I couldn't explain the way my hand shook as I lifted it to the door handle, or the way my heart raced like a manic hummingbird. I tried to shake off the feeling. Just a missing phone. But I bit back a whimper caused by something sinister in the air and opened the closet.

For a split second, the world froze. All was silent. Light filled my vision.

Then, a buzzing started between my ears. My head spun. I took a step backwards to avoid the sickening thud of one hundred and twenty pounds of flesh slamming into the floor.

Within seconds, people leaped out of their seats and toward me. Professor Griffin tried to make his way through the band of students cloistered around the body.

My hands swayed at my sides, feeling weightless, disconnected from the rest of my body, my stomach seemed to exist outside the tiny space allotted it beneath my skin, filling with everything in the room, with a heaviness that threatened to bury me under the thin linoleum floor. I was positive of what I'd seen, yet wasn't quite sure what was happening, couldn't believe in the truthfulness of it. I looked to the ground behind me, to the same place everyone else was looking, I could see a swirl of something that I would have sworn looked just like Chelsea's thick mahogany hair spread out on the floor, even if it was matted in places. I turned without a thought and pushed through my classmates. Reached down to touch that beautiful hair. What was happening here?

"Oh, God," I heard someone say. Someone with a deep, teachery kind of voice. "Oh, God. Chelsea."

Chelsea? No. Why would he say her name? She would be here soon enough, making up time, laughing at herself, her slowness, her unusually lagging schedule.

But then Professor Griffin turned the body over and even with the pale, bruised skin I could see who was lying on the floor. Air flew from my lungs. Empty chest. No oxygen. I felt arms around me, tight, pulling me away from my best friend.

"Get back," I heard. Someone screamed. Then someone else. Spots burst before my eyes, bright spots against a black background. Chelsea? Oh my god. That was her on the ground. Her body and her hair. And her face but it looked so strange and I had never seen her looking so strange before. That's my best friend on the floor, I told the thick air around me with lips that wouldn't move and sound that wouldn't form.

We couldn't move, like wax figures in a horror museum. But it didn't last. There was a sound. A loud, high-pitched one. And I was pretty sure the newest scream that pierced the eerie silence, when I thought back on this moment later, was my own.

2

They sat me in a chair. Asked me if I would like a glass of water.

Their words, the sounds they made ran together into sentences that became incoherent the more they uttered them. The classroom was empty of students, teachers. I didn't know this particular room, this building. I'd never had a class in here before. Next door the police had set up shop. Brought bags of heavy things, investigators, dogs. The ambulance was gone by now. I wanted to go home. But they asked me to stay. The woman. Tall red-headed woman. And the taller bald man. He looked much nicer than her.

You were Chelsea's best friend.

Yes, that's me.

They rushed for a bucket as nausea overcame my stillness. Gave me a moment to wipe my mouth.

When was the last time you spoke with her? Saw her?

She left the party after I did last night. Said she'd see me at home.

Is it common for you girls to party on a night before classes?

We were celebrating.

I hear your kind do that a lot.

We were celebrating a successful fundraiser. For *children with illnesses*. It's the sort of thing *my kind* do a lot.

Miss Sawyer, don't you want to help us find whoever did this to your best friend? We need you to help us out here. Not to get snotty.

The walls were lined with posters of Germany. The Berlin wall crashing down. Neuschwanstein castle. An old church. A river. I'd never taken German.

Another sorority girl–

Her name was . . . flipped page.

Heather. She said Chelsea was talking to some boy last night. Do you know who it was?

She talked to lots of boys. She has . . . had lots of friends.

They looked at each other, Red and Baldy.

Miss Sawyer? Did Chelsea say she was going anywhere else yesterday evening?

They say that German is one of the easier languages for English speakers to learn. They share a linguistic history or something. I'd always thought German sounded rather guttural. But then, I'd hardly ever heard it spoken. Maybe I should rent more foreign films. Chelsea could watch them with me. That was the sort of thing she liked doing.

Miss Sawyer? We'd like more information about Chelsea's plans. Was she planning on meeting someone last night? A friend perhaps? A boyfriend?

Chelsea didn't have a boyfriend.

A pretty, popular girl like that? Are you sure?

Yes. She told me everything. No boyfriend.

She hadn't had a boyfriend since she stopped seeing that guy from USC. It was too complicated, too far to bother with a relationship. They'd been rather casual, broken it off after New Year's. But they were still friendly. I don't know. She didn't bring him up much anymore. It was the kind of friendly that meant that they didn't feel the need to either bad mouth each other or chat on random afternoons. Indifferent friendly. I wondered if he had been German. He was blond. Aren't a lot of Germans blond?

Okay, no boyfriend.

There has to be something you can think of. Someone who—

Stop asking that!

A pause as they considered my outburst.

Looks like that's all we'll be getting out of this one.

Her story is the same as that other sorority girl.

Heather.

Right, Heather.

There was a list. A list of words on the wall. I didn't understand what they said, but it looked like a spelling list I might have gotten back in first grade. Were these the words the class had to memorize for the week? Could I memorize them, if I sat here, all week, and stared at them? Ärgerlich. Eigensinnig. The words sounded good as I bounced them off the walls in my head. Chelsea had spoken Spanish, had said she'd taken it in high school because she thought it would be easy since she grew up speaking it, but it wasn't as simple as that, was a different type of Spanish than hers.

Miss Sawyer, we have to search Chelsea's room. We understand it's your room, too.

I thought about what my dad would say to that statement. To the idea that they will be going through her things. Maybe my things.

You have to have a warrant.

That will be arranged, Miss Sawyer. We just wanted to let you know beforehand. Here is our card. Call us if you can think of anything that would help us find who did this to your *best* friend.

I felt them press something into my hand. I closed my fist around it.

You do want us to find the person who did this to your *best* friend, don't you, Katie?

I stood. Because someone was tugging on my arm, making me stand. A poster of an old, frazzled-looking man watched me take a few steps. Some old German guy. A musician, maybe. A genius of some sort. I knew who it was, I did. But I couldn't think of his name.

Let's go home, Katie.

Carolina's black hair in my peripheral vision. Her eyes puffy and pink. Her fingers guiding me toward the door.

I remembered that they had asked me a question. The mean redhead and the nice bald man. A question about what I wanted. That last thing they had said to me.

Yes. I forgot to tell them. Yes.

She was my best friend.

Was.

Was?

Is. Oh please, is.

3

Chelsea Mathis didn't just have the best hair in the entire Delta Gamma. No, she was so much more than that. She was super talented, a great scientist and the most amazing friend anyone could ask for. Really, she was the type that was even nice to the mean kids and the stoners.

So I don't understand how she could have ended up in the chemistry closet with that puffy blue-tinged face and wide-open eyes like the girls from horror flicks. Who would have done that to her? And why didn't the school shut down, why didn't the world's spinning come to a stop the moment her body was discovered, the way *my* world stopped spinning, the way *my* functions shut down? *Who said life could go on, who would do that to me?*

I tried to convince Dad to let me stay home on Wednesday—*home* home, the house I was raised in up in the Hollywood Hills—but I think he was afraid of me being alone with that scene of a body tumbling to the floor playing over and over again in my mind. He figured I needed to be with my friends. People I could talk to about this. And that seemed weird to me, as though I was being pushed down a tunnel I didn't want to go in.

That night, I stood in the hallway upstairs at Delta Gamma, an uncharacteristic chill whispering over my bare arms, unable to recall having driven the familiar route from my house to the sorority, parking my car in my reserved space, dragging myself, my bag, my keys through to the room I shared with Chelsea.

My feet balked, growing too heavy to move. My sisters — seniors who'd known me forever, lower classmen who'd known my spotless reputation forever — paused like characters in a freeze frame, hands on half-eaten food, mouths in mid-sentence, legs on their way down the hall. The room sizzled around the edges with a thousand unasked questions, worries, fear. I understood. There was a killer out there, and he, she, *it* had targeted a DG girl.

My breath quickened. They stared, silent, waiting to see how Katie, their president and leader and, more importantly, best friend to Chelsea, would react. How I would promise that they would all be okay.

It was like that time I was six. Summer. A hot one. I spent every day outdoors, back and forth between my house and my neighbor, Josh's. I stopped, one time, on the path between our houses, the one with the spaced pavers, squatting, gathering a bunch of his mom's poppies, until I felt tickles on my legs. Scurries and stops. I looked down; my feet and legs were covered in red ants.

I said nothing, didn't move, my fear and surprise shocking me into stillness. Until Josh came around the corner. He saw my legs, the ants that would bite, bite, bite. The scared girl.

"Don't move," he said. "They won't bite if you don't move."

He ran off, but in that moment, the ants were real and I was real and my skin was real and vulnerable and going to be eaten completely.

I screamed. Screamed and writhed and the ants poked and pinched at my feet and legs and hands as I swiped at them. Josh came back with the hose and sprayed me down as I danced and screamed. Then he held my hand and sat by me as I cried while my mom rubbed medicated lotion on my skin.

I felt the ants again, alive in those girls' eyes watching me. How many would take pity on me for losing it, right now? How many wouldn't forgive me for being fallible?

I lifted my chin, just a touch, and forced my feet forward. If I screamed like I wanted to, they might bite.

"Safety," I began, before my throat dried up. I cleared it and started again. "Remember the buddy system from kindergarten? Use it from now on. Take care of each other. *Always*."

I climbed the rest of the stairs and dropped my things outside my bedroom door and went downstairs to be with my sisters, all of us sitting in the living room, holding pillows for dear life, and saying nothing. Most of the girls cried. Some silently, some too loudly. I was too shocked to move. Too scared to accept what couldn't be true. My dry eyes itched like a thousand ants had bitten them.

I waited for Chelsea to walk through the front door, but she never did.

I met Carolina Wu's eyes and she immediately got up, followed in swift succession by almost every other girl in the room. They came toward me, sat next to me, stood behind me, knelt on the floor in front of me, and put their arms around me.

I was like a chick soothed by her mother's wings with all my sisters holding me. It felt good, and wrenching, and like I was going to fall apart. These girls caring so much about me. About each other.

Until, finally, someone said something.

"I heard it was really gross, wasn't it?" Stacey Thompson pulled her legs under her butt as though settling in for some gossip.

"Oh my God, Stace, ask like it was something that happened on the news," Carolina said, her voice catching. "Chelsea was our friend. A sister! The whole thing just makes me sick to my stomach. I can't even eat. And knowing there's someone out there who could do this? I'm scared."

Sophomore Diya Salvatore brought me a cup of tea but I waved it away. My stomach ached like a boulder was stretching its walls taut. I hadn't been able to cry yet. And every time I closed my eyes I saw the most horrible images. They followed me around. I went over the conversations we'd had before she died over and over again, searching for some clue. Searching for my best friend.

"I love that color lipstick on you," I'd said before class two weeks ago.

"Thank you, darling. I know it would horrify you to hear, but it got it on sale."

I faked a gasp, then giggled. "Just tell me you're getting gorgeous for my sake and I'll let it slide."

"Maybe it's for your sake," she'd said, sashaying her hips in my direction. "Maybe I want you to have something pretty to look at in bio other than cultures. Or . . . maybe not."

"Oh, a secret science nerd lover, dear Chelsea? Out with it. No secrets from me."

"Science nerds? No, K, nothing like that. But something secret? We all have secrets, don't we, K?"

"So then who –"

"Oh, hey, we're late for class. Let's go."

"Katie?" Stacey said, biting her lip. Uncertain. "I asked you if you thought Professor Griffin did it?"

"*What?*"

"She fell out of his closet. That's pretty suspicious, don't you think?"

I blinked at her, trying to come to terms with the idea that she was human and yet still asking these questions. How could she, any of us, even think about how Chelsea died? How could anyone have accepted it, yet? Believed it had actually happened instead of being one long nightmare we couldn't wake up from.

"Why is that suspicious?" Carolina cut in, tugging on her black braids. "Between the teachers and admin and the janitor there must be a dozen people with keys to his classroom."

"Even students have keys," I whispered, thinking about my own set in my backpack. Professor Griffin had given them to me so I could work on my labs after hours.

"Okay, so why that classroom then? There are a million places to hide a body on campus."

"Stacey! How can you call her that? A body?" I was glad Carolina had picked up my end of the conversation. I couldn't look at Stacey. Why was she doing this?

"Sorry! I guess some of us deal differently. I'm just trying to think like a police officer. Someone did it. But you're probably right. Professor Griffin is way too hot to be a killer."

Carolina's glare could strip the paint off the walls. "Is there a certain look you have to have to be a killer?"

"Have you seen those America's Most Wanted photos? Sad. It's like people go crazy cause they were ugly kids or something."

I clutched the mug Diya had set on the table next to me, a sudden desire to pick up the whole table, the whole couch, and slam it across the room, crack the windows with the same pattern of tears that were dissecting my heart. School, the whole world, should have been cancelled today. Who would want to be here now? Who could possibly make herself walk into the chemistry lab and not picture bodies lurching out of the microscope closet one after the other?

"Hey, Katie?" Stacey tried again. Lightning flashed. I wanted to bust her nose. I'm so not violent, but right now I couldn't keep it in. And it took me by surprise.

"What, Stacey? What do you want from me? What do you need to know now? Who touched her dead body first? Cause I can't remember that. How about whether her skirt flipped up as she fell to the floor? Cause, thinking back now, I'm remembering that it did. But I don't think anyone was looking at her panties, really. We were rather drawn to her discolored, bloated, *drowned face*."

Stacey and Carolina and Diya and the rest of the girls stared at me with shocked expressions. Yeah, maybe I had yelled the last bit of that. And maybe I was supposed to be the one who always stayed calm. But that didn't mean I needed the sidelong glances that the girls shared with each other as though they thought I was crazy.

Stacey folded her arms across her chest and looked at the floor. I shoved my keys into my jeans pocket and stood.

"K, she just wanted you to take one of these," Carolina said as she folded a piece of paper into fourths and slid it into my back pocket with a soft pat. Her eyes were swimming with tears. "You might need it."

"Sorry, Lina," I whispered. "Thanks, but I have to go."

I made my way out of the house and across campus to the long, sloping front lawn of the school, pressing my palms against my thighs. I thought back to what I had learned in freshman year yoga class. The one Chelsea had insisted we take after our real classes: I paced my breathing, sought my center, breathed some more.

There were trees on the lawn, one, two, three, four of them. I breathed in as I counted the first, out for second. There, two ins, two outs and everything is slow again. Settled and tidy, like a playroom in a catalogue, all perfect bins and unseen content. I didn't deal well with abandonment. That wasn't something I needed a therapist to tell me; it was easy enough for me to figure out. First Simon, then my mom, and now Chelsea. The people closest to me, the ones I'd given myself to wholeheartedly. It became harder and harder to let anyone in, when they were going to leave me, in the end.

Okay, I'd said, the morning after Chelsea put on her new lipstick color. *Today, I'll do your hair for your secret lover. You don't even have to reveal his or her name. I'll ask nothing in return except for you to love me.*

I totally love you, K. You know that.

Groups of students lounged on the grass in little circles. Couples made out in between bites of wraps or pretzels. A trio of tanning girls, their white teeth flashing between their weirdly orange-brown skin, laid back on the slope, facing the dying rays of the sun, their shirts pulled up to display their midriffs. I sat not too far from them and rested my forehead against my knees.

What just happened back there? Who was that girl with the big outburst?

"Yeah, she just *fell out*. Yan told me he heard it from someone who was walking by the room when it happened."

"Oh my God, I totally would have passed out!"

"Me, too."

I had this overwhelming urge to snarl at the girls. But then another one of the flaming Cheetos piped up, shielding her eyes from the sun as she spoke.

"Could we just drop it, already? I can't hear my music with you two chattering away right next me."

Maybe her motives were a little self-serving, but at least she shut the rest of them up.

The girl who would have passed out, a face I didn't recognize, turned toward me. We locked eyes, but she couldn't mask her blatant interest in my reaction to their conversation. I smoothed the anger-wrinkles from my forehead and gave her a neutral look. I was a DG. I could be cool.

The first girl settled back against the grass, "I heard they're doing the autopsy *as we speak!*"

The other two girls gasped in unison.

"Oh my God, can we drop it about Chelsea Mathis, yet?" the girl with the iPod sputtered, glaring at her two friends. "She was one of, like, a million people who go here."

No, I told the girl silently. *Not one* of *a million. One* in *a million*.

"Fine. But aren't you worried? Any of us could be next."

"I'm not worried about it. I'm not in a sorority, so you won't find me stumbling home like a typical drunk idiot sorority girl, just waiting for someone to nab me." The girl who would have passed out looked at me again.

I raised my middle finger slowly and deliberately and turned away.

Yeah, Chelsea and I were sorority girls. But that didn't mean we were stupid. Or any one thing those outsiders could pin down.

The thing about Chelsea, though we all loved her, was she struggled to fit in, I think. She was beautiful, and even though all of us DG sisters are pretty smart, she was the real brain of the operation. And, I don't know, maybe the heart, too.

She had a thing about saving puppies and kittens. And people. She was always bringing us some bit of current events or political info and asking our opinion on it. And when we all looked at her with blank expressions she sighed with exasperation and caught my eye with an ironic smile.

Why mine?

Because one day, back in freshman year, after we had discovered we were two pretty girls with brains in our heads—science-loving brains—rushing at the same house, she looped her arm with mine at a party, all unexpected-like, and grinned at me and told me I was the best friend she'd ever had. Three weekends of laughter and drama and we were best friends forever.

The idea of her so close scared me a little back then, but it was a new start for me. I'd closed the door on other things in my life and needed a breath of fresh air like her to help usher in the new Katie.

So why had she been keeping secrets from me? Or was there really no secret lover, no secrets at all I could tie into her...death. Neatly explain away how someone could take her from me and rip my own heart out. I'd always had an overactive imagination.

I guess I'll never know now.

4

Somehow I got back to my room, although I'm not sure how it happened. I remember snapping at my sisters. And I remember the suntan trio. Next thing, my shoulder was being shaken gently and someone was whispering my name.

"You're going to be late for classes," Carolina said quietly.

I opened my eyes. My body was curled up on one of the downstairs couches.

"I couldn't go there," I said. "To my room. To her room. Our room."

"I know." She sank down next to me and wrapped her arms around me. "It's okay. You can crash in mine if you want. Like you said yesterday, we need to stick together."

"I don't know what to do without . . ."

"I feel like it's surreal, still. Like she can't be gone. Like she's just out for the moment, but she'll be right back."

Carolina paused, because it was my turn to say something. To confide in her. To heal together. But trust didn't come easily to me, and the last girl I'd been able to confide everything to was dead.

"I know." I hesitated. "Could you . . . grab me an outfit? Doesn't matter which one."

"Sure."

I took a shower and pulled on the gray dress with red poppies Carolina had pulled from my closet. I knew I wouldn't be able to go to classes, but I had to get out of the house. I wandered around campus, crossing over to frat row. The air felt different. Like it was charged with static electricity. Fewer people walked alone. More people checked over their shoulders. If this could happen to Chelsea Mathis, it could happen to anyone.

Things felt different this side of campus, too. After all, the last time Chelsea was seen was at a frat party. Police cars were parked at intervals along the road. They talked with guys coming out of their houses, making notes on little notepads. My chest clenched as I realized the killer could be one of them. A cold rush of fear dashed through my veins. Why had I come over here alone? I stopped in front of the Triangle House, prepared to turn back, but paused.

I only knew one person in the Engineering, Science and Architecture frat: Josh Hunter. Just as I thought his name, the Triangle door opened and a tall, slenderly muscled boy strode out like he hadn't a care in the world. He stopped at the top of the steps when he saw me standing on the sidewalk, his expression composed. His hazel eyes flickered in the sunlight. He hitched his backpack up his shoulder, his fitted tee bunching up slightly to reveal the bottom of his toned abs.

Abs I knew well. A body that had, once upon a time, made mine sing. Whose touch sent shivers down my spine and woke up all my senses. I took an involuntary step forward. If he noticed the way he still affected me, after all these years, he didn't let on.

He came down the stairs, said a quick, "Hey, Katie," and brushed past me.

So much for the kid with the hose. The one who made sure I was okay when I'd been certain nothing remained of my skin. I should have known better. I watched Josh walk away, something heavy caught in my throat, then turned around and went my own direction.

#

With Chelsea gone, someone had to fill in at the Greek Week Fundraising Race meeting. Every spring, the fraternities and sororities teamed up for an epic fundraising campaign. The ones who raised the most money got to co-host the Spring Ball.

We do a lot of fundraising. Most of it competitive.

I considered sending Carolina, as my vice president, but would the other houses think we were weak—think I was weak—if I didn't go myself? For the sake of my sisters, who needed a strong leader right now, I went.

The mood at Phi Delta Theta, who we teamed up and won with last year, turned somber when they saw me enter. I gave everyone a weak smile to show them I was okay.

Josh Hunter was one of the last to make it. He nodded at me and took a seat against the wall. I was surprised to see him. I didn't realize he was Triangle's Philanthropy Chair. No, that's something Chelsea would have known.

He stared at me as the minutes of the last meeting were read. A little hello would have been pleasant. Especially since we lived on the same street and had gone to the same schools our whole lives and we used to hang out around my pool all summer long. Since we'd, once upon a time, known each other more intimately than anyone else. In every way. We were fumbling teenagers, exploring each other's bodies on sweltering summer evenings. We were confidantes, sharing secrets, afterwards.

Before things changed. Before we came here. But no, he just watched me all moody-like, his sea-storm gray-green eyes shadowed, as we debated cancelling the Fundraising Race, in light of what had happened to Chelsea.

No, they all decided. We still needed to do this. In Chelsea's memory, our Race dedicated to her.

I wasn't paying attention to the debate. I was focusing so hard on pretending to not see Josh watching me, pretending that his gaze wasn't causing a slow heat to build in my neck, that I didn't hear Colin Branderson call my sorority the first time, either.

"Delta Gamma," he said again. "Chel—I mean, Katie."

My head snapped up. "Sorry. What?"

"Your turn to draw your partner."

"Right." I stood and reached into the bowl of names, scanning the faces of the fraternity representatives. Any one of them could have been at that party. Any one of them could have known something. I closed my eyes to keep from searching for the barest hint of guilty expressions. I couldn't do this. Start being afraid to live. When I pulled a paper out and unfolded I, I frowned and passed it to Colin.

"Delta Gamma and Triangle!"

The rest of the representatives applauded, but I turned and, finally, met Josh's eyes. His gaze swept over my body slowly and the heat in my neck exploded over the rest of my skin. I closed my eyes, trying to escape the way he made me feel, but all that did was let memories rush in to take the place of the dark space: Josh's hands on my legs, his breath behind my ear, the perfect weight of him over me. I practically threw myself in my chair to escape him, tucking my hair carefully behind my ear as I fought for composure.

After the rest of the Philanthropy Chairs picked their names, Colin said, "So, we'll dismiss this meeting now that everyone's paired up. Next time have your event plans finalized and ready for presentation. This meeting is now adjourned."

I rose slowly, smoothed my skirt, and walked over to Josh. He folded his arms across his chest and tipped back on two legs of his chair, smirking. God, that face killed me. I wanted to smack it and kiss it at the same time. "Nice pick."

I folded my own arms and frowned. "We're doing a fashion show to benefit the Humane Society of Los Angeles."

His chair slammed back on all fours and my own smirk grew at his surprised reaction. "Excuse me? We don't want to do a fashion show. And we're supposed to plan together."

I put up a hand. "This has been planned for months. No way you can win with last minute planning. We're having a fashion show so deal with it. Me and Chelsea—"

My voice wavered and my thoughts swam, not connecting smoothly. I was having a hard time coming up with the next words I wanted to say much less actually being able to speak them with the lump forming in my throat and the liquid collecting behind the dam of obstinacy in my eyes. Did I put on waterproof mascara this morning? I simply couldn't remember. I hoped I had.

"We've already contacted designers," I choked out. My hands trembled and I couldn't make them stop. There was nothing to do but cease speaking.

I stared at the far wall, studying the photos of past house members, counting them, breathing. Thinking about how the way Chelsea and I had stayed up late the past few weeks planning for this event might have been considered cheating. Events weren't supposed to be planned yet. But we had always been competitive. Always wanted the edge.

And if we were going to keep an edge, I, everyone, needed a strong Katie. I stood up straighter, stiffened my shoulders and gave Josh a crinkly-eyed smile.

"Just think, there'll be hardly anything for Triangle to have to do. Easy, and a sure win."

I went back to my chair and gathered my bag, intending for the conversation to be over. When I headed out, Josh lingered in the doorway, encroaching on the solitude I desperately craved.

"Katie," he said, and the softness in his voice was like a warm blanket. Damn him for always being able to do this to me, to make me feel this way. Like he and I, together, were some kind of home. But I'd moved out of that home years ago and I needed the door to stay closed.

"What do you want, Josh?"

"Sounds like Triangle could do a lot, actually," he said, folding his arms and leaning against the doorjamb. He filled the doorway. I'd forgotten how much space he seemed to take up. Not that he's particularly tall or overly built. Really, his height was just about perfect and he played soccer, so he was fit. But the simple fact of him just took up space. Maybe it was his attitude. It was so big. Or his ego. "Building a stage, engineering lights and sound, making it a real production."

"Yeah, okay do whatever. Just leave the heavy lifting to the ladies."

Josh laughed at me and didn't budge.

"Always acting like you're better than everyone else," he said.

"Always reminding me why I stopped talking to you in the first place," I shot back.

The grin fell from his face.

"I have to go," I said, pushing past him. "Move."

But he wouldn't.

"We'll help with the other stuff, too. Just let me know." His face softened a little.

I eyed him warily, fighting back the urge to tear up again. What other stuff did he mean? Other show stuff or . . . other Katie stuff? I recalled, again, how sweet it had been to share secrets with him under a starry night sky. He stepped toward me and I cleared my throat. Same Josh as always. No, I couldn't do this. Didn't he get that I'd moved on long ago?

"Thanks, but you'd just be in our way."

Josh's face darkened.

"Dammit, Katie, you are so difficult. I was trying to help. You used to be so— You know what, never mind. It'd be a bitch working with you anyway."

I glared at him, wishing I could sock his smirk off his face. Oh, it would feel so good. Not that he wasn't right, in a way. I used to be different. The kind of girl that welcomed his help.

Maybe I should be able to, now. Maybe I should have gotten over everything that happened between us years ago.

But maybe…it still hurts to think about losing the people I loved the most. Maybe it was easier to compartmentalize everything into cupboards and close to doors to the mess inside.

I brushed by him.

His next words caught up to me as I reached the bottom of the porch steps.

"Hey, Katie?" His voice was gentle and questioning now. He had come out and was standing with his hands in his pockets, looking at me intently, but uncertainly. He was so different from Damon. The way he held himself with casual grace, the way he understood . . . too much. All my emotions stood at attention when he was around. It reminded me why I chose to be with Damon. It was less complicated. "I'm really sorry about Chelsea, you know. I wish it'd never happened."

Without the darkness hiding my face, he would have seen me crumple. Instead, he only saw me rush away.

5

Damn Josh. He had *no* right to bring that up. I was getting through the meeting just fine without having to be reminded, without having my concentration slaughtered by the knife of his concern. And now I couldn't just go back to DG house, all droopy eyes and shaky mouth, the sad doll Katie incapable of putting on a face, a smile to let everyone know it would be okay.

Halfway across campus, I pushed the door to Young Hall open, intending to hole up in a lab until all my quivering passed, but the sight of the crime scene tape across the lab doorway gave me pause. I started to turn around, then caught sight of a paper taped to the wall.

The paper was purple, a pale purple, like the lavender color of a fine French lotion. The same color of the paper Carolina had stuffed in my back pocket. I perused the one on the wall as I pulled the other one out of my pocket. It was a flyer for Dr. Marsha Cleary, Campus Trauma Specialist, who would be here at the end of the week to talk to students affected by Chelsea's death. Sign-up sheets for the thirty minute long sessions were in the student services building. I unfolded Carolina's paper and glanced over it quickly. It was the same flyer.

I sighed and leaned against the wall. So maybe the girls hadn't meant to be horrible. Maybe they just thought that I could use someone to talk to.

I popped into the ladies' bathroom, setting the flyer from my pocket onto the counter next to the sink as I leaned over to spit the yucky taste from my mouth. I turned the water on and let the coolness run over my hands and into the sink, then took a drink and spit again. The drains were thin or clogged, or something, because the water was taking a really long time to drain. The sink filled a third of the way, then halfway, and I couldn't take my eyes off the clear pool.

But I forced myself to look away, to look up into the mirror. And I wasn't the only one looking back at me.

I spun around, my hair flying behind me, and searched the bathroom. There wasn't anyone there, but I swore there had been, my thoughts weren't so far gone, so close to craziness as that, were they? I bent down and checked under the stalls. No shoes. The doors all swung open tentatively as I pushed on them, one at a time, looking for a figure, a body. Nothing. Blood pounded through my veins and throbbed in my head like a drum. I knew, I knew, I knew I saw something behind me. I wasn't insane. A girl, a friend, a shadow. A ghost?

A killer?

But no, the hair was just the right color. She was just the right height. And the smile was the same, the same encompassing brightness, the one she always gave me, hers, my favorite, oh God.

The water still ran from the faucet like a miniature waterfall.

"Chelsea?" I croaked, biting back laughter the moment the name touched my lips. I breathed, focusing on slowing my heart rate and gathering my shattering nerves back off the floor. There was nothing there. Nothing, nothing there. I leaned over, cradling my face in my hands and let myself giggle. Like a madwoman.

Stopped.

Forced myself to stop and breathe.

This couldn't be happening. Not Chelsea gone or me barricaded in the bathroom like a cracked egg. I forced myself to look in the mirror. Admit I was alone. Always alone.

But okay that way.

It was impossible to say how long I would have stayed there had not the sound of cresting and seeping water torn me away from my reflection. I looked at the sink and watched the water fall over the sides, droplets bouncing off the floor and onto my shoes and splashing my perfect dress.

I grasped the faucet handle and yanked it into the off position. I eyed the flyer.

I crumpled it into a ball, tossed it in the garbage, and slid my headphones over my head, the sounds of my favorite indie rock band drowning out thought. Chelsea was always admiring my taste in music. I remembered when Courtney Dreger rushed for DG and I told Chelsea we had to have her, because I wanted a cool musician in the house.

I love that about you, K. That you want to be friends with everyone, that you want DG to be so well-rounded, she'd said. *You make everyone feel like they belong here.*

I twisted my mouth at the woman staring back at me in the mirror and wondered if spending so much time making sure everyone else was taken care of meant that I didn't spend enough time taking care of myself. My thoughts flickered back to Josh. Someone who always could help take care of me. Back when we were together, I took care of him, too. But in that way...that mutual love kind of way.

Chelsea had become that person for me after Simon died and my mom took off and I kicked Josh out of my life. But she was gone and I had no one. I shook my head. I had Damon. He would be out of his class by now. I sent him a text on my way over to the house he rented with a few of his football teammates.

Need you now.

His came back immediately.

I'm here for you.

Damon's "here" wasn't like Chelsea's. He didn't have to listen to my secrets. He just had to soothe my hurts away with his hands. And fifteen minutes later, standing there, on his porch, with his shirt off, his sharply defined muscles being cooled by the early evening air, I knew I'd made the right choice. He was hot. Everyone knew it, but only I got to act on it. And his focus during times like these, when I was throwing myself at him, was single-minded: pleasure.

Exactly what I needed. Nothing to think about but his hands on me.

"Hey, babe," he said, tugging my bag off my shoulder and pulling me into his chest. We didn't have reason for any other words. He bent down and kissed me, pressing his mouth against mine forcefully, just the way I liked from him. I dug my fingertips into his back, rounding them on the backs of his shoulders, clutching at him. A quick, roaring fire built in me, strong enough to burn all the thoughts, all the feelings that were threatening to crush me.

"Let's go inside," I said against his lips.

Damon turned me against the wall next to the door, the wood digging into my back with the right amount of pressure. I lifted my chin as his mouth moved lower and he dragged his teeth down my neck, bit into my shoulder, raised my arms and pressed them to the wall over my head. It became a playful struggle, trying to get inside while he caged my body in. His kisses came faster, harder in a way I knew I'd be feeling tomorrow morning. Each one sucked away another piece of my thoughts until all I knew was the need to get up to his room.

I slipped my fingers out of his and drew them lightly over the front of his shorts. He was as ready for me as I was for him, his hardness pressing into my hand for more. But I denied him.

"Upstairs," I demanded.

Damon flung the door open and we tripped over the threshold, then stumbled up the stairs.

"Out," Damon commanded to whoever was in his room. I heard the shuffle of papers, the darting away of footsteps, but didn't see who it was. I didn't care. This was what Damon did best. Take my mind off everything. The stress of taking care of a houseful of girls. The demands of my classes. The hurts that followed me to college. And now, my best friend, gone. No talking, just movement.

He threw me across his bed, tearing at my clothes. We undressed, flinging shoes across the room, our hands moving blindly, fiercely at each other. When I thought he was going to lie beside me, he seemed to change his mind and dropped lower, his tongue tracing down the center of my stomach, going further, flicking at my clit. Pleasure rushed through my legs like an ocean wave. I pressed my head into his pillow and closed my eyes, so glad to be taken away from everything haunting me.

But another face greeted me when I closed my eyes. Watercolor green-blue eyes and a mischievous smile. I snapped my eyes open and stiffened.

"That was quick," Damon said, raising his head with a slow, dark smile.

My heart was racing, my body cooled suddenly, my muscles clenching in protest.

"Yeah," I gasped through a fog. *Go away*, I demanded my thoughts. But they kept peeking through the fog that was burning off in my mind.

"Success." Damon looked pleased with himself and it didn't surprise me. He had a hard time getting me to climax. It wasn't him, I knew. It was that too often, like this time, the mental fog that made going to him such a temptation cleared just enough to let emotion through and I just . . . couldn't. Usually I faked it. It wasn't fair to him to feel like he wasn't doing something right when he was doing exactly what I wanted. And it's not like I didn't enjoy all the lead-up.

But this was the first time I'd seen another face. A familiar face. A face that knew my body at least as well as Damon, and my heart even more.

I struggled to lock away my thoughts as he put on a condom and arranged my body in a sideways position he knew

I liked. I pulled him to me, but only really came back into the moment after he was finished.

He rolled to my side, settling in for an overnighter, but I got up and put my clothes on. My body was tense with frustration.

"I have to go," I said, distractedly, walking out of his room and house alone.

#

The DG house was full of nervous chatter the next morning, everyone making their best guesses as to who could murder a woman, who could hold her head under water until she fell limp like a broken doll. Who could prop her up in a chemistry closet. Because her body didn't get there accidentally, her heavy, liquid-ingested limbs didn't move on their own.

I had made it to my classes barely on time, following the directions to the new classroom for my morning lab that were sent in an email, and somehow stumbled through the first half of my day. I couldn't remember taking notes. My filing system, the one that put everything into neat little brain-boxes, seemed to be taking a vacation.

Damon met up with me for lunch, sitting behind me on the grass, rubbing my back between my shoulder blades. I smiled at him appreciatively. These were the things he was good at. The simple things. He liked his hands on my body and I liked massages almost as much as I liked sleep.

"You can pay me back later tonight," he whispered in my ear suggestively.

Despite his attentions, by the time afternoon rolled around I was tired and headachy. And I knew it wasn't fair to my sisters to be sullen and introspective when we were all going through this together, so I tried to keep my smile on at the house, to assure them all that the Katie they knew and trusted to be steady was still here.

"The sisters want to do a memorial thing," Carolina said in a subdued tone at dinner. She poked at her salad, but didn't eat it. I eyed her, but it was like I had started a trend yesterday and now we were all avoidy with one another. Our glances flicked to the darkening windows, wondering if the person who'd gone after Chelsea was out there. Tension clouded over the room. "They wanted to run it by you."

I nodded slowly.

"And if you had any particularly favorite pictures you wanted to contribute or funny stories or mementos or anything . . ."

I had a million pictures. At least. But I didn't know if I wanted to share any of them with everyone else. Chelsea thought it was a hoot to take pictures of herself in her underwear. Not in a pervy way, just goofy. And there was no way those were getting out. I had been saving those for when she was on some big reality show and needed a scandal to help boost the ratings.

And funny stories? I had a million of those, too. But they were even more sacred than the pictures. Let them call me selfish. I was fine with that. I was just not interested in sharing a side of Chelsea only I got to see.

"I don't know what I think about this memorial thing," I told Carolina, trying to keep a quiver out of my voice.

"I mean, people need closure. And to understand what happened. Something to help them remember. Eventually . . . a way to start moving on. Especially with the killer still running around out there. The girls are hardly sleeping."

She was right. Madison Taylor had purple circles under her eyes and Diya Salvatore was wearing the same wrinkled shirt as yesterday, as though she'd not-slept in it. Even so, it didn't sit right with me.

"And that's all going to come from a bunch of people standing around holding candles?" I whispered to Carolina. "There is nothing to *understand*. She was murdered and nobody knows what really happened."

"People have all these questions and sadness, though."

"So, what? Are you going to post a line-up of suspects next to her picture? A list of evidence? Everyone can pick their favorite possible murderer? Professor Griffin. Or maybe Terrel Watson. Because he thought she was cute and she turned him down, so why not? Or maybe you could get some quotes from the detectives. A picture of them posing over Chelsea's body. How about a lock of her hair glued to a program so that every person in this school can feel like they have a piece of her?"

Carolina looked away and I stabbed at my food.

"Sorry. I just –" Carolina waited for me to finish, but I didn't even know what I wanted to say. Get it together, Katie. I closed my eyes, just for a moment, and breathed. The smile I gave Carolina was thin, but her relief was almost instant.

"They're questioning all kinds of people," she said, grasping to a change of topic. "The detectives, I mean. It's all over the news."

"I haven't been watching." No, I'd avoided T.V., the radio, the internet: everything. A beautiful, popular girl falls out of a school closet? It had to be all over the place and I didn't want to hear what sordid theories people who knew nothing could come up with. "But I saw them over on Gayley. Are there any leads?"

"They talked to Professor Griffin, but he has an alibi, I guess. They're talking to Chelsea's parents and Charlie was on the news trying to get away from the reporters."

"Oh, God, poor Charlie."

"You two were together all the time. Is there anyone you can think of?"

Anyone who would want to kill Chelsea? Not a chance. To know her was to love her.

I shook my head. "Fanboy obsession?"

Stacey pulled up to the table with her dinner like she was some kind of car taking a turn too fast and parked herself into her spot. I watched her take her first bite and chew it slowly, watching us the whole time with an "I know something very interesting" look on her face. But I wasn't going to be the one to bite.

Stacey let loose a soft sigh every few seconds, her fluffy pink vest rising and falling with her chest.

Any other time, the way Stacey tried to get our undivided attention made me laugh. She loved stirring up drama, and usually it was harmless. But I didn't have patience for her habits now. Not about this. I sighed. "Just tell us, Stace."

"Okay, so you know how my brother's high school pitching coach is the brother of the secretary at the sheriff's office?"

No joke, Stacey knows *everyone on the face of the planet*.

"Well," she continued, "this morning she was waiting for a new applicant to fax in their resume when another fax comes through and she intercepts it. Guess what it was?"

"People still use fax machines?" DeeDee Brown asked, crossing her long, dark legs and leaning in to the conversation, celery stick held high.

"Another application for the job?" Carolina muttered.

"Of course not. You won't believe what it was, though. Guess again."

"We don't want to guess," Diya cut in, rolling a cherry tomato around with her fork. "Just tell us."

"Spoilsport," Stacey said with a pouty lip. She tucked in close, over the dark wood table, her shadow cloaking everyone sitting across from her like the dark shadow of a villain. "It was an autopsy report." Her statement ended like it was a question, but I think she figured out that we would give her a bloody nose if she said guess again because she leaned back quickly and didn't demand we 'guess again.' "It was Chelsea's autopsy report and I know what it says."

My stomach revolted as I listened to her talk about it. I stared at the pattern in the wallpaper and tried to think of something to say. About my best friend. About what they had to do to her body to determine how she died.

Carolina saved me from having to say something. And, I had to admit, it was the thing I wanted someone to ask.

"What did it say?"

"That the cause of death, based upon the fluid found in her hyper inflated lungs, sinuses and airway, was drowning."

We let loose a quiet groan all together.

"We already knew that, Stace," Carolina said. Her eyes flicked to me quickly, then away again. "Some of us here *saw* her."

"Don't jump all over me, okay? There's more than that. I just wanted to start at the beginning and give you all the facts."

Stacey took a breath. Even she seemed shaken up. Usually, she was more like a bulldozer, all energy and no hesitation.

"There were bruises and scraped off skin on her ankle. And there were all these scrapes on her fingers but not like she was fighting someone . . . unless they were sandpaper. It was as though she tripped and drowned or was fighting against a wall to escape, or something. Or maybe someone was trying to scrape her skin off. Like that guy in Silence of the Lambs who needed all that skin for his costume thing...." Stacey paused when she realized what she was saying.

Carolina turned her head away, but I was caught by Stacey's words.

What did Chelsea's ankle have to do with drowning? And her fingertips . . . was it her fighting back, was it a water-holding container that wasn't smooth on all sides? What did her killer do to her body before she was dead? I got to my feet, a bit dizzy and a lot overwhelmed. My fingers tingled and my hands shook as I stood there, not saying a word, everyone looking at me. Again.

I picked up my dishes, forcing my hand around my knife, clenching it into a hard fist.

"You're not leaving, are you K? I wanted to tell you something else. I'm positive the murderer was a guy. A classmate, maybe. Want to know how I know?" Stacey paused, slowly looking at each of us in the eye. "She was pregnant."

6

The news traveled quickly through the Greeks even though every DG girl swore they didn't tell anyone about it. As for me, I wouldn't share that secret with anyone.

But what really killed me was that Chelsea didn't share that secret with anyone, either. I didn't even realize she was seeing somebody. Did she even know she was pregnant? How long had she been? If she did know, how could she have kept that piece of news to herself?

Chelsea told me so much about herself that I thought there was nothing else to tell. I heard about her mom's muumuu obsession, her dad's struggles to make ends meet, her older brother, Charlie's, boyfriends. She even told me about the time she made out with another girl during the summer between high school and college when she was backpacking through Europe.

I thought those were big things. But this was huge. Life altering. My mind went over everything she said and did in the weeks leading up to her death. Thinking about the way she'd felt, what she'd said. Any clues she might have dropped. She was sick, but we'd thought it was a stomach bug. Now, my own stomach clenched painfully at the thought of what it really was. Chelsea was good at taking care of herself. Surely she'd notice if her body felt different. And if she'd known...why would Chelsea feel she couldn't turn to anyone about this? Why couldn't she turn to *me*?

I would have helped her. I would have done anything to make things better.

By the end of the next day my confusion had become debilitating, leaving me standing in the middle of Dickson Court in some creepy sad-girl daze, going over every possible way Chelsea could have been drowned, every possible person that could have killed her. Terrel had been quieter than normal in the new chem lab we'd moved to, pushing his glasses up and turning away whenever I looked his way—did he have something to hide?

The only person that didn't strike me as out of sorts was the one person I knew wasn't capable of killing more than a bunch of ants.

"Watch where you're going . . . please," I said, when Josh Hunter bumped into my elbow as he sped down the grass backwards, catching a Frisbee from some unknown person behind me.

Josh froze, then pulled back as though I was sending off electric shockwaves. He tossed the Frisbee back, stuffed his hands in his pockets and looked me over.

"Sorry about that," he said as he moved a little closer to let people pass through behind him. "Didn't see you there."

I had the sudden urge to brush his hair out of his eyes. Instead, I said, "Obviously."

"You waiting for Damon to come get you?"

"No," I said, staring up at the fluffy clouds. Wishing I was in them. Anything to be lost, to be unseen. "Not that it's any of your business."

He raised his hands in the air, palms out, in a show of defensiveness.

"You could hang out with the ice cream truck man, for all I care. But you were the one standing in the middle of the grass looking at nothing like some lost zombie. I just figured if I helped you find your way you could eat Damon's brains instead of mine."

Huh. As if Damon's brains could supply any zombie with a complete meal. We made the perfect couple, but underneath that muscled rich-boy exterior? Suffice it to say, he's not headed off to med school anytime soon.

"Are we done here? I've enjoyed our chat, but I have so much to do." I gave him a vacant smile.

Josh's mouth hung open as he peered into my face, so close that our noses were almost touching. It took everything I had to not react, to remind myself that we weren't the same people we used to be, the same *us*. That we weren't anything, anymore.

Because the way my heart was racing, my skin coming to life, being so close to him, was telling a different story.

"How do you do that? Just turn off like that? It's amazing. That level of crazy. It's like you stood in line for the psycho superpower. No . . . The Great Emotional Vacuum Girl. And congrats, you got it!" He pulled away again and flicked his fingers at me. "All right, SuperSucker, off you go."

I had to pretend he didn't exist. Pretend he never existed.

I didn't need him.

I breathed and turned away.

"Katie!"

Every part of me wanted to ignore him. And yet, I turned.

"What, Josh?"

"We need to get together soon. Go over fashion show stuff." He pressed a sticky note into my palm. I felt his touch not only in my hand, but across my breasts, trailing up my skirt. I remembered the way he used to slide his fingers into me, his mouth covering mine, my hips rocking to a rhythm he set. I clenched my teeth together, trying to banish him from my memory. Trying to banish the sudden, fierce wanting in my body. He didn't seem to notice the effect he had on me. "Here's my cell number," he said.

I looked at the paper. Josh had written his name and phone number. Like a stranger would. Under that he drew a little picture of a dog face. I had to smile, for real this time, because under the dog face he wrote two sentences: *I know you like the dogs better than the fashion. Can't fool me.*

"Oh, and Katie?"

I looked up. He was only paying half his attention to me. The rest was watching for the next Frisbee toss.

"Superpowers? I stood in line for flight. How awesome would that be? Zooming over everything. Didn't get it, though. Just not as lucky as you, I guess." He threw his arms up in the air with a wry half-smile and chased after the disc in the air.

#

No, I hadn't been waiting for Damon to pick me up that afternoon. I was waiting for the house to clear out for the ice cream party. As I'd predicted, Delta Gamma had won our little bet with Chi O over the Spring Carnival preliminary fundraiser and it was time for them to pay up. I was supposed to be there. I'd told Carolina I'd be a little late. Things to do.

The DG house was deserted.

Just as I wanted it to be.

I headed for my room. Our room. I'd gone into Chelsea's closet countless times to borrow clothes or grab her textbook if she'd forgotten it. I'd left notes on her corkboard and presents on her bed. I'd never gone through her stuff behind her back. Never gone in to rummage, search for parts of her life I wasn't involved with, things that . . . I don't know what. It felt wrong.

But I needed a project. This project. The only one that could heal this massive bruise expanding across my heart. I needed to know who killed my best friend.

The police had come in to look around already. I don't know what they left with. It all looked normal. Like before.

The corkboard was decorated with an assortment of bumper stickers. The funny kind, like "Nice truck, sorry about your penis," and the serious kind, like "Club a baby seal today?" It was home to Chelsea's photos. The two of us sticking our tongues out at the camera. The two of us making kissy faces at Damon and him looking like he'd hit the jackpot. Charlie. Her mom and dad. Old wedding photos of her grandparents. We both had agreed her grandma had been a stylish babe in her day. Good genes were so important.

She'd lined the back of the board with aluminum foil, laughing the whole time, calling it a poor girl's mirror. We'd giggled at how distorted we looked in it. But there were no clues tacked to it.

I caught a whiff of Chelsea's perfume as I held the door to her closet wide. She didn't actually wear it on her body much, but she left the bottle on the shelf where the scent drifted faintly over her shoes and dresses and scarves and permeated them with the delicate Chelsea signature.

On one side she'd stuck one of those self-adhesive hooks to the wall and hung bracelets and necklaces. There were three necklaces on it now; one was the BFF half heart I had given her two years ago. I pulled it off the hook, listening to the chains tinkle against one another like cartoon fairy dust. I pulled the necklace over my head and pressed the pendant to my chest for a moment.

Breathed.

In between it all was a stack of books. Her chem textbook, *My Antonia*, a library book about democracy and capitalism. Around the books, a package of sour gummy worms that I eyed with a smile, but left alone. A nearly empty bottle of water.

I knew I shouldn't feel like I was snooping, not with how close we were.

"Hey K," she'd always say from the bathroom or downstairs. "Go in my closet and grab my books for class, would you?"

"Okay, but I'm going to see all your dirty underwear you've shoved in the back," I'd say. "I won't defile your shrine to Angelina Jolie."

"Aw, K. You could never defile it. Mi casa es tu casa and all that."

I poked around a little more, tipped up the books and checked under them, glanced at the ceiling of the closet hopefully.

"Are there no clues in here, Chels?" I said to her shelf of shoes. "To help me figure out who did this to you? A phone number I wouldn't recognize, a picture, a pair of dirty boxers, maybe?"

When I still didn't see what I was looking for, I clutched the door handle. I knew my tampering could get me into trouble, if anyone knew I was in here. Although, surely the cops had taken what they needed by now.

On her corkboard, a photo of us caught my eye. We were in Tijuana, carrying big straw bags, shopping. She'd taken me down after a particularly bad weekend, when the past reared up at me and I needed to get away. Chelsea was so great for that. Listening, hugging me, then taking us somewhere. In the picture, I looked at the camera with a broad smile, one arm around Chelsea and the other holding out one of the little soapstone elephants we'd just bought. She had her head tipped back, her lips kissing the sky. I pulled the photo off and slipped it into my nightstand.

I pushed the door closed. I heard the latch click into place.

Then headed down the road to be sociable.

7

It was a place that moved: the receptionist fidgeting behind the counter, the navy-clad bodies streaming back and forth behind her, the people in the lobby tapping their shoes as they filled out report paperwork or waited to pay their speeding tickets. Sound and space and matter streamed by me at a speed that weakened my knees.

"You need something?"

The receptionist tilted her chin my way and looked at me with eyes that could bore a hole through a cement wall. I suppose if I had to wear a uniform that made me look like a petrified tree trunk I'd be pretty ticked off, too.

"I need to see him, please." I passed the business card across the counter and took a step back. There was a smell here that made me want to turn and run. Something maybe coming from the prostitute lounging against a side wall or from the unshaven man hunched into his filthy blanket on the bench. My arms crawled, but I had to stay. For Chelsea.

"Do you have an appointment?" the receptionist barked. I cringed.

"No. He told me come see him if I had anything to tell him."

"Right. Take a seat. We'll get to you."

I surveyed the lobby for acceptable seating. There wasn't much to choose from. I finally decided on a chair next to a respectable-looking man in a dark suit about my dad's age and sat, propping my bag on my lap and giving the man a quick smile.

"What are you in for?" the man asked out of the side of his mouth. His breath smelled like old cigarettes. I leaned away from him.

"I have to speak to a detective."

"Oh yeah? What'd you do?"

"Me? Nothing at all. It's about an investigation."

The man's right eye twitched and he leaned closer to me.

"What'd you do?" he asked again. "*What'd you do? WHAT'D YOU DO!*"

The man stood, inching taller with each raised decibel. He loomed over me, fists tight. Shouting came from every corner of the room, filling the tight space. I yelped and wacked the man over the head with my bag. He man fell back into his chair with a high-pitched cry as two officers rushed into the lobby and led him into another room. The receptionist eyed me with a wry grin and shook her head.

I lifted my chin and smoothed my skirt in place.

Then the red hair.

"This way, please." The detective, the woman, beckoned for me to follow her down a hallway.

My limbs seized up on me.

"Oh, is the other detective not in today?" My voice sounded small and tinny to my ears. I felt like prey. The detective wrinkled her nose and tried not to smile.

I rose from my chair and took a breath. *Be brave*, I told myself. Be strong. Invincible. No fear.

I followed the detective down a hallway filled with people and bulletins on the walls and sounds and shouts and the smell of microwaved soup and hot dogs. I tried not to gag, but the smells combined with the way everyone I passed looked me over, like I was a naughty schoolgirl, sent waves of queasy over me.

I didn't do anything.

I don't get in trouble.

"In here. Can I get you some water?"

I entered a small room with a messy desk on one end and shook my head. The detective followed me in and pulled a file out of a cabinet before sitting behind the desk.

"Have a seat."

I watched her open the file, saw the photo paper clipped to the inside cover, noted the thick stack of papers within. I swallowed. What did they already know? Were they about to make arrests? Who? If I just knew who, I could leave this place, let everything go back to normal.

"Is that Chelsea's file?"

The detective raised cool eyes to me and sat back in her seat with the file in one hand and a pen in the other.

"So, what can I do for you, Katie? It's Katie, right?"

"Yes."

She made a note in the file.

"Right. Katie. Kind of tough to get to cooperate, as I recall."

I tore my eyes away from her, both of us knowing I hadn't been terribly cooperative. But who could be, moments after discovering her best friend's body?

The wall behind the detective was covered in paper. Certificates, newspaper clippings, a county map. Faces of convicts stared back at me with eyes that spoke murder. Red and blue, green and yellow tacks held it all in place. There wasn't a bit of white space behind it all. Was it one of those faces who did it, who stole my best friend from me?

"Katie?" she prompted.

The window, a tiny square to my right, was open. The breeze blew back the curtains in a flowing rhythm. It fell over me, the coolness. I hated the detective. Hated that someone wasn't in jail yet for what he did to Chelsea.

"Miss Sawyer? I don't have all day. I have work to do. Like solving Chelsea's murder. You like wasting my time?"

I cleared my throat and clutched my bag against my chest.

"I heard something."

The detective sat forward again and pierced me with her stare. She tapped the tip of her pen against her desk.

I continued. "Chelsea was pregnant."

"How did you know that? Had you known all along? A secret someone told you to keep? It's a crime to withhold information from a case like this, you know."

"Yes, I know that. And no, I'm not keeping anything from you. Or anyone. I was pretty out of it that day. What I'd just seen, what I'd—" I paused, expecting to find a measure of pity in the detective's eyes but she looked back at me with the singular piercing of an endless tunnel. There was no empathy for me.

"Okay. Let me rephrase that. If you have information, I'd greatly appreciate hearing it. I've seen quite a bit myself, Miss Sawyer. Enough to know that it's tough for girls. That people need to learn violence against them isn't okay. Enough to know that I want to put away anyone who thinks murder is an answer, you know?"

I nodded. "I want to put him away, too. I want to know who got her pregnant."

"Ah, now we're getting somewhere. Because I do, too. That's a pretty big piece of the puzzle. So if you have any information, I'd like to have it."

The detective leaned forward and fixed me with a steely look.

"I wish I had more to tell you," I whispered. She nodded and relaxed slightly.

"I wish you knew something more, Katie." She bent over the file.

"Actually," I said, interrupting her note-taking with a strong, clear voice, "there was one more thing. The scratches on her ankle?"

"How do you know about—"

I cleared my throat.

"Everyone knows. Anyway, they weren't there before." I closed my eyes. "I mean, we'd gotten ready for the party together. I would have noticed something like that."

The detective studied me for a moment. "Thanks for the tip. It's something we're looking into. Maybe it'll give us a clue to where or how . . ."

She twirled her pen between her fingers and let her eyes drift to her wall.

"You take it seriously, violence against women, don't you?"

She looked back at me, her eyes piercing. "Very seriously. If you have anything else to help us...?"

"No. Just...I appreciate it. Your dedication."

She grimaced. "Thanks. It's not a nice world out there for us. Anyway, I'd better get back to making it at least a little bit nicer. I'll find someone to show you the way out."

I stood and squeezed the handle of my bag in my fist.

"It's okay," I said. "I can manage. Look, I realize you're the pro, but she was my best friend. I'll do anything . . ." I swallowed down the anger, the frustration. "Just . . . just find out who did this to her."

8

I slept in on the day of the memorial, wordlessly watching Carolina get dressed and leave. I knew I needed to get up, myself, but I just couldn't drag myself out of bed. My dreams had been dark the night before and there was no spot on the bed that could make me comfortable. My back ached and my neck hardly supported my head anymore. I sighed and thought about what to wear to the memorial. Whether I could manage to go in the first place. I needed someone else to hold my hand and tell me what to do.

"I knew you'd come," Josh said, waiting for me in front of his fraternity. "I knew you needed me."

"I don't want to need you," I whispered. But I still took a step toward him. Then another one.

"I know." He came closer, holding a hand toward me. I took it and it was like he could suck my tension away through his fingers. My shoulders relaxed and I let out a long breath. "But for once…for right now…let yourself go, Katie. After, we can keep pretending none of this happened. None of us happened."

"Yes. That's exactly what I want." He tugged me gently and I pressed my body against his. Swimming in the warmth and scent of him. "Just a little time to let go. No strings attached. Can I really have that, Josh?"

Instead of answering with words, his hand went to the back of my neck. I raised my eyes to his and told him, silently, that this was okay. It was perfect. His fingers tangled in my hair as he lowered his lips to mine...tenderly teasing the tension and pain out of me. I let him have control, but as my body softened under his, a new energy filled me. Desire took the place of everything he was releasing from me...I wrapped my arms around his waist... urging our kiss to a new depth.

I remembered this. All of this. The feel of his thigh alongside mine, our breathing in time, quickening as our hands searched familiar places. I slipped my fingers under his shirt, tracing the lines of his lean muscles and he moaned quietly against my mouth.

"I never stopped missing this," he murmured. "I was a fool to let you walk away."

"Shh. I'm going to leave again, after this, remember?"

"For now, then, no walking." Josh swept his arms under my legs and lifted me off my feet, carrying me into the frat house and to his bedroom in the back. He arranged me with my head on his pillow and everything in this room was so much *him* that I had to force myself to not cry. The soft cotton pillowcases that held the smell of his skin, the slightly rumpled, pale green duvet, the cleats and dirty socks in the corner, the haphazard stack of books and papers on his desk, where I knew he studied as hard as I did.

But before I could get too emotional, his hands were working a path under my shirt to cup my breasts. He lowered himself next to me and worked his lips over my neck, behind my ear, over my shoulder. My shirt came over my head and he buried his face in my chest...I reached for him, but he pushed my arms aside and rolled me onto my stomach. His teeth dragged across the back of my thighs, over my hips, up my spine.

"You are still perfect, Katie," he said.

I started to shake my head, but he caught my earlobe in between his teeth. I smiled. Luxuriated in his heat. "I'll believe you. But only right now. Only because this is a dream."

And realizing that woke me up. I sat up and looked around. Discovered I was still in bed at the sorority, my blankets tangled around my knees. I'd fallen back asleep after Carolina had left. The late morning sun was soft across the walls, but my heart raced. I grabbed a pillow and pressed my face into it with a maddened scream.

#

The ladies were subdued at dinner. Carolina sat quietly and fiddled with her baked potato. DeeDee stared off into the distance and ate her orange absently. Even Stacey was quiet, erratically divulging her snippets of gossip in whispers that probably no one heard, had anyone actually been paying attention to her.

Damon showed up after dinner, looking like a lost little puppy. Guilt about my dream consumed me. I realized I'd been pretty brusque with him over the last few days and that it would totally suck to have a girlfriend going ballistic when he was so used to her cool calmness. What was he to do with me?

I could make an effort, put on a good show, if nothing else.

"Hey," I said softly. He put his arm around me and I scooted closer.

"Missed you earlier," he said. "It's quiet today. All depressing and shit."

"So you're glad to see me then?"

He looked me up and down, taking in my black skirt, my gauzy black top, my black headband. I even painted my nails black. He cleared his throat.

"You kind of look like a vampire. But other than that, yeah, I'm glad to see you. I need you to look over my Com assignment from Monday."

I stared at him. "You could go in and see a tutor."

He nodded at me as he passed me his paper. "I know but...you're the smartest person I know. You and all your . . . covalent bonding thingies that you're into. You know, the uncool kind of bondage."

Despite the way I felt like the sky was pressing on my chest, I snorted. Damon wasn't perfect, but he made me laugh. "Chemical bonds are cool. They hold important stuff together. Look it up."

"Okay. One of these days I will. If you'll look up the other kind of bonds." He flashed a bad boy grin and I had to give him a tiny smile.

"Maybe I will." He didn't know that I already had. In another life, with another boy. Josh and I had been so trusting, so comfortable with each other that we'd explored. Discovered things we liked and didn't like. Had secret passions we—at least I—have never shared with anyone else. I knew the cinch of rope around my wrists and ankles. And I knew how to tie them, too.

But that life was over.

I pressed a kiss to Damon's lips. His hands traveled over my hips slowly. "I always get what I want, eventually. People like us always do. Whips and chains and—"

"God Damon, shut up," Carolina said from behind us. We'd left Delta Gamma and started walking to the Court of Sciences, where the memorial would be held.

"That girl needs to get laid," Damon muttered.

We walked silently until we got to the Court. I took his hand as we entered the throngs of people gathered. Pains shot through my stomach. All these people, but they'd never even known Chelsea.

"The family funeral's tomorrow," I said. "I hope you're coming with me?"

Damon raised his head and looked across the courtyard. He checked his phone before answering me.

"I'm thinking about it. But I have football . . ." Damon's crazy busy sports schedule generally worked for me. He trained with the next year's team, even though he was graduating soon, and that left me with a lot of time to focus on my studies. But now, I almost felt like I could use him with me. On an emotional level. Maybe that was a bad idea. Especially since we were graduating soon and moving on to our new lives. He looked back at me with a gleam in his eye.

"You don't have to go to football," I said.

"It's a brotherhood thing."

"And Chelsea was like a sister to me."

"But the guys—"

Carolina breezed by and grabbed my arm, rushing me forward. She turned her head to him, glaring. "Shut the fuck up, Damon. Now's not the time to be such a . . . *boy*."

Damon's expression changed into something like an apology. But he still didn't change his mind about Chelsea's funeral.

#

The memorial was held at sundown. Hundreds of people were gathered in the Court, and that made me unreasonably angry because hardly any of these people actually knew her. And only the tiniest handful of us *really* knew her. And, even though I thought I knew her better than anyone else, I was coming to realize that maybe I didn't know her at all. So that meant that nobody knew her.

I figured out that no one had consulted with me about the memorial when Diya took a microphone hooked up to tall speakers and led us in a moment of silence. Then, Dr. Cleary from the science department rose to address us, delivering a sonorous speech about how the death of a fellow student affects us all, even if we weren't friends with the deceased and how it can really affect the morale of school, how it could make us question who we were and what our place in the world was and how we all needed to pull together in this trying time, come together and heal together. Then she talked about how we could also turn to our families and our personal belief systems to help us through this tragedy.

I closed my eyes briefly as Diya took the mic again and issued an open invitation to the crowd to come forward and share their feelings in an appropriate manner.

A silly thought occurred to me and I stifled a giggle because the court had gone dead silent. I should go up there. I should grab that mic and turn this into a rollicking karaoke scene. Throw down some terrible summer pop anthem or some classic country twang. Chelsea would have loved that. The only things she took seriously were her politics and stuff.

"Maybe some heavy metal? Huh, Chels?" I whispered under my breath, thinking about all the music I'd shared with her over the years, how I would burst into our room with a new discovery, make her quit her studying to listen. She always said my music lifted her mood.

"That would be the funniest thing ever," she would have said, now. Instead, I only got the memory of the sound of her voice, soft in my mind.

I closed my eyes and reveled in it.

"Who's that?" Damon said, looking across the auditorium at a girl making her way to the podium. I opened my eyes and looked to the figure he nodded at. She was tiny, this girl, but cute. I squinted at her, trying to make out who she was and how she would know Chelsea. But I came up with nothing.

"Beats me. I've never seen her before today."

"Hi," she began. "My name's Mel and I just wanted to come up here and talk about what's in my heart right now. I didn't really know Chelsea like some of you did, but I felt like I knew her, you know? Like when we were at the same party and she caught my eye, I just felt like she was looking right at me. She had that way about her, as though we all mattered and we were all significant. I never had a class with her because I'm a freshman, but I'd always heard about how smart she was and when I heard she'd died I just felt so sad, like this light has gone out of our school. She was one of us and she made me feel like I was one of you, too."

Oh gosh, did she really? You who probably didn't know her name before this? Mel went on.

"This is a great opportunity to come forward and set our souls at ease," she flashed a simpering smile to Dr. Cleary, "and wish Chelsea the best as her own soul moves forward to Heaven."

I almost gagged. And then, when she walked away from the mic and I saw that there were six more unfamiliar faces waiting their turn, I did gag. My eyes became watery and my nose filled with snot and I made this horrific retching noise.

This Court, so full of people. So full of people who could have killed Chelsea. Wide eyes and narrow eyes and sad faces and bored faces staring at me.

"Damn, K, are you all right?" Damon checked his jeans to make sure that I hadn't actually slobbered on him, but it was clear. Nothing was coming out.

"I've got to go," I gasped out between sucking in breaths. I rose and stumbled out of the crowd, pushing through people, sounding like a herd of elephants as I moved. The person at the mic paused in his adoration of Chelsea and everyone watched me almost fall on my face as I stumbled away.

"Whoa there," said a voice as Josh's hand reached out to steady me. My body jerked under his touch.

"I'm not a horse," I sputtered into his face. He dropped my arm and I stumbled on, gasping for air. Outside the crowd, I pulled myself up tall, smoothed my skirt to mid-thigh and brought control back to my expression.

Katie Sawyer.

I was Katie Sawyer, Delta Gamma president, and they needed me to be cool. I walked from the Court, forcing each step to slow, to be normal, to be controlled.

9

I went back to the DG house and to bed after my brilliant exit from the school memorial, waking with the sun on the morning of Chelsea's funeral. Carolina dozed across from me and the house was quiet, but I felt antsy. I dressed and skipped breakfast, then got in my car, squeezing my steering wheel and gazing into the endlessly blue sky, not knowing what to think about that time after the funeral when people get together and talk and mingle and laugh and catch up with relatives they haven't seen for hundreds of years as though the most important person, the one who brought them together and created their shared ties, wasn't gone.

I headed down to Sunset and just drove for a while, switching albums on my playlist until I found the right words to match the way my soul stung. The road was winding, but mostly clear since there weren't a ton of people driving around this early on a Saturday. It felt good to coast, to have nothing else to focus on but the way my foot felt on the accelerator and how the wind felt through my hair.

I kept driving when Sunset ran into the Pacific Coast Highway, heading north until the houses faded away and were replaced by the brown Southern California mountains that, poor things, tried so hard to be green. I made a split second decision, acting as though I wasn't headed here all along, and pulled off at Topanga Beach, settling into a parking space.

I kicked off my heels and pulled my hair back into a ponytail with an elastic sitting in the cup holder, tiptoed across the parking lot, then relaxed once my toes had sunk into the warm sand. The granules cooled as I moved closer to the waves, the raw chill travelling from in between my toes to my ankles and calves.

I loved the beach. Really, truly loved it. The sounds the waves made as they rushed in to shore and crashed against the land. The widespread wings of the white gulls overhead, searching for a meal, fighting each other at the garbage cans. Triangular sails in red and white bobbing out in the distance. And the smell, that briny but fresh and clear, ocean smell.

Nobody bothered you on the beach. They jogged by with their dogs and waved or ignored you as they sun worshipped or maybe just passed a friendly nod as they trudged through the sand, their wetsuits dripping, their boards gleaming in the sun. It was a place to be alone without feeling lonely, my favorite place. I didn't know what I'd do next fall when I began grad school in the bay area. Beaches there weren't the same.

Here, I could admit there were a lot of things I didn't know. How I would feel without my dad close by. How I'd get on without Chelsea with me. How unsettled I still was from my dream about Josh. I tried to hide all my worries in front of the sisters, but the future was . . . a scary place. It seemed doable when I had someone to face it with. Now, it loomed like a giant wave that I had to decide if I would ride like a surfer, or drown under.

I walked for a time then sat on a smooth patch of sand next to a rock. The sea occasionally reached my toes, lapping them gently and companionably. I used to come here a lot more a few years back, before life became so busy with all the things I was supposed to do. After my mom left and . . . after Simon. It was a good place to relax and think, or not think, if that's what I preferred. To put things back together. To file and compile and reevaluate and delete.

Even now, as the thoughts of people who were gone, who had left, who couldn't be saved, piled in on top of one another I could wipe them all away with one look at the breathtaking scenery up the beach.

My finger dug a little hole in the sand as I remembered a girl who used to always sit next to me on the beach.

"I love the beach," I told her, avoiding her gaze.

"I know. You tell me that every time," she said, with tenderness in her voice.

I leaned back against the rock with a sigh.

"What are you doing here? Do you really want to sit there while I moan about poor little me? I really shouldn't. I'm lucky! I have so much!"

"I just wanted to be with you for a while, is that okay? I want to listen. That's what best friends do. Maybe everyone else thinks you're perfect, but I know better. I know how much of a slob you are."

She tried to make me laugh, but I shrugged and watched a yellow Lab run past. Its fur was wet, spiky, and the dampness showed off the movements of the muscles underneath its coat.

"I miss them," I whispered, my voice drifting past like a wisp of breeze.

"I know, K. I bet they miss you, too."

I sat up at her words, frustration taking hold of my insides. There wasn't anything I could say about Simon, but my mom? "Then why doesn't she ever come back for me?"

Chelsea gazed out over the foam capped waves. "I don't know. She's missing out, though."

"Missing out on mopey Katie."

"Then come on," she laughed. She rose to her feet and bounded right into the ocean, splashing through it with the force of a train. "It's cold!" she screamed at me, throwing her arms out like a bird and twirling under the sky. She dived down under the waves and stayed there for a full minute, surfacing again further out. "You should come in!" she yelled, motioning to me to join her.

She looked behind her, judging the next wave as it built up. She dived again, this time towards the shore, and rode the wave all the way in, ending up with her belly on the packed sand. She pulled herself up, water dripping from her clothes, her thick hair. She settled back in next to me and I could feel the cold of the ocean radiating off of her like an aura.

"I would," I teased. "But I don't want to shame your terrible body surfing with my hot skill."

She twisted her mouth at me, her eyes twinkling. There was something else behind that twinkle. Something deeper. "And yet . . . you're the one drowning."

My stomach tightened into knots and the sand particles in the air burned my eyes. I dropped my face into my hands. Abruptly, I got to my feet and touched the rock for balance. I knew what she meant. All the times I'd gotten her up at three a.m. when I couldn't sleep and needed to get away or when I wasn't able to sit through class because the buzzing in my head was too much and I had to take off. She knew my secrets. The way people had left me, how I wasn't strong enough to create opportunity for more people to leave me, how I always held parts of my heart back, too scared to lose them. To lose more of myself. And yet, I let her in the way I couldn't let anyone else in. But she didn't let me in. Now she was gone.

And that kills me.

10

Chelsea's funeral was that afternoon. The real thing that people who really knew and loved her were invited to attend. The one with family that, considering the size of her Italian father's family and her Hispanic mother's family, would fill Our Lady of Hope to the rafters. I couldn't say I was looking forward to it, exactly, but at least it would be nice to be among like-minded folks.

The Mathis home was a sweet little cottage set back from the street and surrounded by weepy willow trees and tulips. It was something out of a fairytale, like that little place Sleeping Beauty stayed in out in the middle of the woods when she wasn't being a princess and had to do all her own cooking and cleaning.

It was still surprisingly quiet when I got there late that morning, but I supposed the majority of the family was busy setting up at the church. I didn't have to knock, though, because the moment I stepped onto their porch the front door was thrown open and Chelsea's mother rushed outside to grab me.

"Oh Katie, oh thank heavens you're here. If anyone can hold together through all of this it's you." She squeezed me tight, then pushed me back, holding me at arm's length. Her hands shook, were frantic over my arms. "I love you. We never say it enough to people when they're here and when they're gone we wish we'd said it more. But you're a good girl and Chelsea simply adored you."

It took me a second to gather my thoughts.

"I loved her, too. And she loved you." With a deep breath, I tucked stray hair tendrils behind my ear. "Mrs. Mathis, what can I help with?"

"Call me Tina. Oh, I know I say that to you every time and you never do, so I suppose you never will. It's funny. But good. So respectful. You kids. Such good kids." She held the door open for me and waited for me to slip by before closing it again. It slammed too hard, shook against the frame. "Let me just look at how things are going in the kitchen and I'll get back to you. Have a seat, make yourself comfortable. There's magazines. Something. Yes. I'll be right back."

I sat on the couch and watched Mrs. Mathis scurry around the house, moving things from here to there or gathering a series of photos to take to the church. Several times she stopped in the middle of a room, a bewildered expression on her face as though she wondered how she got where she was.

She was nothing like her daughter. Where Chelsea was tall and statuesque, Tina was short and bony. Her hair was always cut close to her scalp and she had a nervous energy that set me on edge. Watching her fuss and pause and stammer now nearly sent me right *over* that edge.

I liked her because she was warm, but her erratic movements made my heart pound painfully in my chest. She needed to slow down. We all needed to slow down. How else was Mrs. Mathis going to be able to heal from this, from losing her daughter? I winced at the pain of a swallow and looked up as Charles, Chelsea's older brother, walked in, pausing in the doorway to let the screen door settle into place without a sound.

Charlie was the spitting image of Chelsea, with his dark hair and underwear model figure. It was too bad that he was never interested in me, or in anyone carrying a uterus and a set of boobs.

"Hey, Katie," he said, his voice somber.

"Charlie." I stood and we hugged. He lifted me off my feet and really powered into the embrace. Then I felt him shudder and he set me down again as he tried to catch the sobs that racked his body. "Oh, Charlie," I whispered.

"Sorry, Katie. I miss her." He wiped his eyes on the back of his dress shirt sleeve and stared at the wall for a long moment. "I'm glad mom has all her pictures on the table and not on the walls anymore because I've hardly been able to walk around the house all week. Every time I turn around I'm staring straight into her eyes."

I let the room settle into quietness for a moment, like one of those minutes of silence that we give to people who have died, as if that one minute was going to heal everything, before I spoke again.

"You've been here all week?" Charlie was a sophomore at UC San Diego. He studied anthropology or archaeology or one of those ologies.

"Yeah. I wanted to be here, with mom and dad. Just..." He wiped again and closed his eyes. He breathed. It was good technique that he used. I smiled at him encouragingly. "It's hard."

I nodded, but I wasn't sure what else to do. Mrs. Mathis still tore around the house like an RC car on auto and Charlie had grasped my hand in his and was staring at it.

"Have you heard?" he whispered. "About the pregnancy?"

I nodded again. "One of DGs found out. It kind of got around. But not by me."

Charlie smiled at me. "Those kinds of things don't stay hidden." He shot a glance at his mother and gave a little pull on my hand. "Come on, I want to show you something."

He led me to the back hallway of the house and stopped in front of Chelsea's bedroom door. He put his hand on the doorknob. "Can you handle going in?" he asked, staring into my face to garner my reaction.

I thought about the last time I had entered Chelsea's room. It wasn't long ago. During spring break as we'd packed for our trip to Baja. Chelsea had painted her nails as I rifled through her closet.

"You know what I love?" Chelsea had asked as she blew on her toes. "I love this, being like this, doing this. Sitting here with you, listening to your music, painting our nails. Like there's nothing else we have to do, you know? Things are going to get so complicated soon and people will be moving and leaving and not seeing each other ever again. All these new responsibilities to worry about."

"Ugh, the real world," I agreed, comparing two pairs of her sandals and tossing them both in her bag, just in case. "Isn't it sad how everything has to change? But I'm still looking forward to it. It'll be fun."

"Yeah," she said, staring down at her toes. "And the Bay Area's not that far, so I'll come see you all the time."

"Don't remind me that we won't be roomies anymore."

Chelsea carefully screwed the cap back on her nail polish bottle. "I know," she said slowly. "I'm thinking about taking a year off instead of the job offer at Hyacinth Tech. Maybe going back to Europe for a little while. What do you think?"

I paused, the polish brush held high. The notion of taking a year off, of throwing a wrench in The Plan caught me off guard.

"But what about the real world? Getting an apartment and starting your career and all that?"

Chelsea giggled. "I know. But I've felt kind of smothered by the great and almighty Plan lately. You can't tell me it doesn't get to you. The stress? We're supposed to figure things out in college, right? But I'm not so sure I have."

I blew on my new polish color and rolled my eyes.

"You're brilliant, studly and, oh yeah, brilliant. What else is there to figure out?"

"Come on, Katie. Lay off the big act." She flipped onto her stomach and caught my eyes with her own. "Even you have cracks in that armor of yours. Take some time off and come with me. One year. What would it hurt? I'm sure you could defer admissions for a year and I promise to load your social calendar with all the parties and amusements you can handle. We'll rent a villa on a lake in Italy or we can get a flat in Paris. Whatever you want. It'd be so much fun. And we're so damn hot that Europe wouldn't know what to do with itself. Come on, you know you want to."

I lifted my chin in imitation of parents everywhere. "Are you trying to peer pressure me? You think that if you jumped off a bridge, I would too?"

Chelsea flipped onto her back. "Ugh! Mark my words, Sawyer, I'm going to get you to come with me."

I'd laughed at her then, but what really sucked is that over that next weekend I started thinking seriously about what Chelsea said, even to the point of shooting off an e-mail to my dad's personal secretary asking her to check into rental properties in Paris and the Lake District. A year break from classes made some sense and parties with French and Italian hotties was the frosting on the cake. But I never got the chance to tell Chelsea I had taken her seriously, and now I wonder if she died thinking I had been blowing her off.

I hadn't known about the pregnancy then, and only now did I wonder what she really wanted the time off for. Was her plan to keep the baby? Stay away for a year to avoid gossipy watching eyes? Would she have given it up for adoption in the end? She talked about new responsibilities...she must have known. A baby was what she meant, right? Why hadn't she trusted me enough to *tell* me?

I traced the pattern of Chelsea's door with my eyes and made myself forget that we'd ever had any plans at all, then met Charlie's gaze and, for the third time in ten minutes, nodded.

He pushed open the door to Chelsea's room and I hesitated, gathering strength, before entering.

Not much had changed since the last time I was here. The nail polish bottles stood on her dresser like soldiers in a line, from palest shade to darkest. That was me – I was a little OCD. Her walls were covered with posters of bands I'd recommended and hot actors and actresses because cinema was more her thing. The mirrors on the walls left little room to actually see oneself, they were bordered with so many photos and love letters. Her bed was made, but that must have been the work of Mrs. Mathis, because Chelsea never, ever made her bed. Her closet doors were open and her shoes were a disaster. Her mom must not have gotten that far in her tidying.

In the middle of the floor, surrounded by candy wrappers and scarves and diamond patterned tights was his laptop, instantly recognizable for the Zippy's Burgers stickers plastered all over it. Charlie was a burger junkie. Charlie picked it up and sat on the bed. He patted the place next to him and I obediently sat.

"The police came through here once earlier in the week, but Chelsea's laptop was in my room because we had played a marathon Jewel Thief tournament when she was home this weekend. She forgot to take it back to campus. I didn't tell them about it, and they didn't ask. Not me, at least." Charlie brushed his hand over the top of the computer. "I wanted to get the first look, you know? Because I felt like I had to know if there were things that she was scared to share with me."

I understood what he meant.

"And then I felt guilty going through her things so I came in here with the laptop so she could show me what I needed to find. Like her spirit guiding me? I know that sounds crazy. Sorry about that."

I gave him a companionable shove with my shoulder. Crazy to want to be in his sister's room when that's all that was left of her? That wasn't crazy at all. Crazy was seeing her face in the girls' bathroom mirror. Oh, yes, I had the market cornered on crazy.

"In the end, I decided it was crazy, yup, so I just copied all her files to my computer so I could go through them slowly."

"But isn't that obstruction of justice or evidence tampering or something like that? I don't want you to get into trouble, Charlie." The detective's hard voice played in my head.

He shrugged.

"What they don't know...and I turned the laptop in a couple days ago. Told them I forgot about it in all the confusion."

He opened the laptop and fiddled with a few things as I thought about his mom and wondered how she was doing out in the front room. Did she need me now?

"Did you know that approximately twenty percent of marriages end in divorce after a child dies?"

I didn't mean to blurt out the statistic, exactly, it was just there, sitting on the edge of my tongue, waiting to make itself known. I ducked my head after saying it, knowing that Charlie was silently staring at me.

"Sorry," I said.

"It's okay," he said. "Actually, I did know something like that." Hmm, maybe his ology was psychology? "But you don't have to worry about my mom and dad. They're not the type to fall apart individually. They'll come together to do that." He paused, pondering. "We're—" He shook his head and choked on the word. "I'm lucky that way. Good parents."

"Must be nice," I said.

Charlie flung his arm around me and gave me a squeeze.

"It's tough having your family torn apart."

He turned his attention back to the laptop and pulled up the files from Chelsea's computer. He opened the list of e-mails archived in the folder and clicked on the oldest one. It was short, just a sentence long.

I must see you again. My place. Tonight?

The e-mail was dated over three months ago.

"Do you think this is him?"

"I don't know," Charlie said. "But it seems likely. All the e-mails are short like this one. I love you, I miss you, I must see you. It goes on like this for weeks until..." Charlie pulled up another e-mail from almost six weeks ago. "This one."

What I said—I'm just surprised. I hope you didn't think I was mad because I'm not. I'm excited. It's going to be okay.

I felt ill as I read the words, ill and hopeful. This was our man, it had to be. Did he know that Chelsea was dead? Has he wondered why she hasn't answered his e-mails for a week?

"What's the last one say?" I asked.

Charlie caught my eye.

"Yeah, that's what I wondered, too. Does he know about Chelsea? Could he maybe know who did this to her or, just maybe, be the one who did it? But I don't know. His last e-mail is almost three weeks ago and it doesn't exactly reek of psychosis." He clicked on the last one in the file.

Chels, don't worry about it. It'll work out. She'll be angry and I'll probably get into some trouble, but it doesn't matter. I love you. I'm going to take care of our family. Just tell me what do now, when to tell. Do you need anything? Write me back.

Our family. He knew. *She* knew.

Chelsea was pregnant and she knew and she didn't tell me. And now she was gone. I swallowed back the rock that was growing in my throat. Coughed. Stared at the wall until my chin stopped trembling.

I passed the back of my hand over my eyes. "That doesn't sound like a threat," I said, quietly. "More like a lovesick puppy pleading his case."

"All the e-mails from that week are like that. And she didn't reply to any of them," Charlie said.

I looked over the e-mails again, my eyes drifting to the username. Sigma2992. I pointed to the name.

"Do you know who uses that account?" I asked Charlie.

"No idea," he said.

I looked at it again, tumbled the letters and numbers around in my head for a while. I knew little about code and so had no idea whether the word stood for something in particular. It sounded kind of familiar, though.

"Wasn't Chelsea's ex in a fraternity? Your friend?" I questioned.

"Yeah, but it couldn't have been him. He's seeing someone else. As for the—" Charlie waved his hand at me, unable to say the word. "We were hanging out with a bunch of people all night Monday. Gaming." Charlie shot me a sheepish look.

"Oh. Okay, but what if she'd met someone else? Like, another guy in his frat who liked her but she shot down? Revenge violence against women...it's a scary thing these days."

"Possibly. I was thinking the 2992 could be a birthday. You know, February 9, 1992. Do you think there's any way of narrowing down who that information belongs to? It would be great, I guess, if someone we knew had that birthday. But realistically, it could be anyone in the country who happens to come to L.A. with some frequency. I don't know how to get that kind of information."

I mulled it over but it didn't take me long to come up with a name.

"I know someone. Give me a few days."

11

I didn't bother calling Josh Hunter. I just popped by Triangle Saturday morning and told the nerdy guy who answered the door to grab him. When Josh showed up, his eyes widened with surprise.

He got a hold of himself pretty quickly, however, and ran his hand through his sleep-mussed hair. For a moment, I saw him again like I did in my dream. His attention—and fingers—fixated on my body. I wanted to be the one running a hand through his hair. But I forced the desire down.

Because that—everything we were and everything we did—was before. And now I had Damon.

"Hey," he said with a yawn. He looked me over, taking in my pink trimmed athletic skirt and my white t-shirt. His gaze felt heavy, slow. Almost the way his hands used to. The force of that delicious memory made me catch a breath. Why couldn't I keep myself under control? The way his eyes crinkled at the corners told me he noticed the way he affected me, still. I scowled and he struggled to hide a sleepy smile. He leaned into the door frame. "I thought you didn't hang around campus on the weekends."

I didn't. Since home—not the DG house, but my real home—was only a few miles away, I usually spent weekends there with my dad. But I never saw Josh anymore—at least, not before we were teamed up for the charity project—so how did he know that?

"I don't. I'm heading off to tennis lessons in just a minute. Then home. Some of us, it appears," I looked pointedly at his scruffy pajamas, "can be up before ten in the morning on the weekends. But then, some of us have lives."

Josh stood politely and listened to my speech, even if he did raise his eyebrows. When I was done speaking, he pushed himself off the door and peered into my face. I couldn't meet his eyes. Not after my dream. I fought to keep a flush at bay, but my cheeks heated up anyway.

"I was up late last night. Entertaining company," he said quietly. Was that a smirk on his face? Did he mean lady company?

It didn't matter. Josh's personal life didn't matter. Today I was in control. One hundred and ten percent effort kind of control. I had a mission. And once this mission was completed, everything could go back to normal. To perfect. I shook his words off me and peeked into the house behind him.

"Are you going to invite me in?" I asked, wondering if last evening's visitor was still hanging around.

She must have been gone because Josh opened the door and stepped aside, bowing slightly and sweeping his arm wide as I entered.

"You don't have to be such a dick, Josh," I said.

He didn't answer me. He just laughed in that infuriating way he had and closed the door behind us. I stepped into the foyer and headed for a couch, but Josh stopped me with a throaty sound and I turned to look at him.

"I was just making some breakfast. Mind if we do this . . . whatever this is . . . in the kitchen?"

I changed direction and headed left to their kitchen, a sparse space hiding under signs of life: mail on the counters, a loaf of bread drying out in an open bag, a wadded-up paper towel next to a half-wiped puddle of water. Boys.

I slid onto a barstool, setting my racket on the granite counter, and waited as Josh filled his bowl with Lucky Charms, topped the cereal with milk and grabbed a spoon. He walked around the island and set his bowl down, seating himself on the stool next to mine.

I watched him slurp his first spoonful.

"Gross, Josh." He ignored me as he took another bite. "You know, when you're choosing your breakfast cereal you should read the nutrition information. If there's more sugar than fiber then it's not a good choice."

"I'll keep that in mind," he said. Josh considered the back of his spoon for a moment before dipping it in his bowl again and taking another bite. This time he splashed milk on the counter right next to my arm.

"Ew," I said. "Why can't you eat like a civilized human being?" I slid off my stool and grabbed a napkin from the holder on the counter, slapping it in front on Josh's bowl. He picked it up and wiped at his milk, then held the dirty napkin out to me. I scowled at him and snatched it away from his fingers, tossing it into the garbage.

"Thanks," he said as he pushed his bowl away and waited for me to return to my stool. "So, what's up? We haven't really had time to build the stage and lighting yet."

I glared at him. "Don't be dumb. This is far more important." I paused, gathering my thoughts. He ate his cereal as if I wasn't there. "Last night was Chelsea's funeral."

Josh abruptly dropped his spoon into the cereal and sat up straight in his seat. A light went on in his eyes.

"The family funeral. You were there. Of course you were there. That had to be . . ." He shook his head as though the right thing to say to me couldn't be found. "I'm really sorry. I'm sorry you lost her."

"You make it sound like I misplaced her. Left her somewhere. I didn't. She—she left *me*." I hadn't meant to say that, but the way he gazed at me, the familiar way he cocked his head to the side and really listened, drove the truth straight from my brain to my mouth. I tucked my hair behind my ears. I would have to be more careful.

His voice was soft. "She didn't leave you. She didn't die on purpose. It wasn't her fault. Or yours. You know that? And not just Chelsea. Simon…your mom."

Josh looked at me intently and his eyes were like tidal pools at sunset. I saw the concern written in them as though it was spelled out with flashing neon lights. I almost told him. Every thought that had kept me up at night this week, every sound that grasped at my chest and made me want to cry. The way I couldn't meet anyone's eyes anymore without tripping over my own feet. The way I was glad her funeral was closed casket because I was *this close* to losing it. And if I'd seen her face?

Gone.

I almost told him the way I used to be able to tell him everything. Him, holding me, the heat of our skin pressed together, and me, whispering my fears in his ear.

But I didn't. I couldn't. Josh was . . . this part of me that belonged sometime else. In another world, in the one before this one. If I wanted everything in that world to stay where it belonged - in the past - Josh needed to, too. I had to move forward. No matter how much I suddenly didn't want him to stay in the past. I cleared my throat and looked away to the dirty socks that sat next to the toaster on the far counter and ignored his question.

"I was talking to Chelsea's brother beforehand and he had been going through some files on Chelsea's laptop and came across these e-mails that she wrote to some guy. We're pretty sure it was the guy she was seeing before she died, but there's no personal information in any of the e-mails. Just a username."

I pulled a slip of paper out of my pocket and passed it across the counter to Josh. "Sigma2992. We figure it's a fraternity related, or something. And a birthday. February 9, 1992. A guy, of course. Chelsea dated a frat guy over the winter. One of Charlie's friends. But he was with Charlie all Monday, so maybe she met someone else at a party? And there was, like, jealousy or something? I don't know. We'd look ourselves, but neither one of us knows much about how to go about looking for people or e-mail users or whatever and I thought about who I knew that probably *did* know how to do that and so here I am."

I looked back at him and took note of the tilt of his mouth and the amusement in his eyes. I renewed my glare. "I'm hoping you can help. Do you think you can possibly be serious long enough to help me out with this?"

"Why aren't you going to the police or hiring a PI for this whole thing?" he asked, picking up the slip of paper and studying it then setting it down and looking back at me.

"The police already have the laptop, but what are they doing? Have they found the killer? No. And I'm not hiring someone because this is private, and PIs aren't private, are they?" It was so hard to be sarcastic when he looked at me that way. When my skin tingled under his gaze. Stop it, skin.

"Uh, actually, I think they are. I mean, it's part of their name and everything. Private Invest—"

I had to cut him off before I whacked him over the head with my tennis racket.

"Okay, whatever," I snapped, "PIs are private, sure, you always have to be right. Fine, you're right. Happy? Can we move on now? Do I ask so terribly much of you? Can you find it or not?"

Josh grabbed my hand unexpectedly and held it in his, pulling the fingers free of its fist and staring at the open palm. I closed my eyes and focused on breathing out my anger, finding my center. But when I closed my eyes I saw his mouth close to mine, his legs tangled with mine, felt the cold of night against my naked back and his hot lips traveling over my stomach, his tongue across my inner thighs, the smell of grass in my nose.

My eyes popped open and I sought out the dirty socks again. Nothing like stinky boy things to cool a girl down. Okay, there it was. My center. Right there. I felt better.

"You don't ask nearly enough," Josh murmured and looked up, catching my eyes again. A shiver fluttered down my arms.

I froze, unthinking, and I almost left my hand there but I just couldn't. I yanked it away from his hold and nearly fell onto the floor in my haste to get off of the barstool. I took a few steps toward the windows that looked out over the little Triangle backyard and stared, unblinking, at the volleyball net.

Then I tidied my skirt and smoothed my shirt over my stomach and turned to face Josh again. His t-shirt was heather gray, with a drawing of a flying squirrel on the front. Fitted enough to see the outlines of his chest and the tops of his slim hips just above where his pajama pants sat. The whole effect was effortlessly sexy. Playful, like Josh. Not like he was now, though. Now, he watched my movements with a blank expression on his face that helped me gather my thoughts, suffocate my emotions and stuff the wiggly little things far, far down where they belonged.

"Just, do you think you can help me with this? I know we'll eventually have to take it to the police." I pressed my hand to my forehead, suddenly confused and unsure of what I was doing. With this information, with so many things. Was I really willing to get into trouble over this? "But I knew Chelsea and I know her family and I know they just want to get past all this without some bully detective asking them a zillion questions, and why haven't they found her killer yet and, just, *please*, Josh."

"You're not worried about getting into trouble?" Josh asked.

I dropped my hands to my sides, unable to keep my shoulders from slumping a bit. He always said the things that got into my cracks. Because he knew where my cracks were.

"I don't get into trouble," I told him. It was true. Trouble skipped over people like me.

I felt so tired suddenly. Like I wanted to crawl up into someone's arms and stay there for a while. Chelsea's arms, maybe. I looked at Josh and he must have seen something in the look I gave him because he began to slide off his stool. I pleaded with him with my eyes. Pleaded him to not come any closer.

"Do you remember—"

"No," I whispered, wishing, wholly and completely, that it *was* his arms. I shook my head. I had a boyfriend. And Josh . . . I just couldn't. "Please. I should go."

I turned towards the front of the house.

"Hang on," Josh said, dropping off the stool completely and reaching into a cupboard for another bowl. He filled the bowl with Lucky Charms and reached for the milk, then hesitated, set the milk down, and pulled a carton of soymilk from the fridge. He poured just enough soymilk in to moisten the cereal then dropped a clean spoon on top and set it in front of the stool I had been sitting in. "Here. Eat this. I'm going to take a quick shower and get dressed because I have to head over to the arena where we're having the fashion show to take measurements." He looked at me thoughtfully and ran his hand through his hair again. I stared back, surprised. He was really jumping into our project. Taking it seriously. Taking *me* seriously. "Want to come? You could check things out. Tell me about your ideas for design elements."

I considered him and the bowl of cereal and thought about how he remembered I preferred soymilk and about how I could probably reschedule tennis. How I could switch lunch with Dad to dinner with Dad.

"Okay," I said as I returned to my seat and picked up the spoon. "I'll come."

12

I let Josh drive because even though I liked to drive I knew guys got all testy about that sort of thing. Men and their control issues. We loaded into his car and headed up the 405. The arena was someplace in the valley so I was lost the moment we crested the Santa Monica mountains and began our descent into the hinterlands.

"I'm glad you didn't put up much of a fuss about what we'd picked to do," I told Josh as we sped by the exit for Mulholland Drive. "Even though it's so far out here."

Josh turned the stereo down so we could talk, but at the speed we were going I could just barely hear him laughing at me.

"It's all of thirty minutes away without traffic," he said, switching lanes to pass another car that was probably going ninety. "And I didn't see the point of protesting. You take pride in always getting your way." He glanced over at me.

I nodded and smoothed my hair over my shoulder. "True."

"How'd you hear about this place?"

"I didn't. Chelsea . . ." I choked and swallowed and turned away from the look Josh gave me. "Chelsea had planned it. She met the vet for the shelter through Professor Griffin."

He kept looking at me. I couldn't see him, as I stubbornly stared out the window, but I felt his stare on the back of my neck, heating it until I felt warmth in my cheeks, too. I wanted to arch my back under his gaze, as if it was his fingers exploring.

"Have you even cried, yet?" he asked softly.

My body went cold. "I am dealing with her death in my own way, thank you," I snapped.

When I faced him again, his eyes had gone all liquid. I'd forgotten how he could do that—could make me feel so cared for.

"That's not what I meant," he whispered.

I knew what he meant. He meant Simon. But that was dangerous territory. My heart was already too fragile at the moment.

"How're your mom and dad?" I asked, desperate for a change of topic.

Josh sighed, but let me move the conversation to something new. "They're good. They're both at a studio rehearsal this weekend. Mom's getting ready to record her next album and Dad's threatening to sing on it."

A low laugh escaped me as I pictured his parents. I knew them well. Josh and I had been next door neighbors growing up, after all. Josh's mom was a talented classical violist and his dad was an armchair opera singer. His voice wasn't terrible if you liked listening to flamingoes squawk. I liked this. Talking about his family again. Settling into the comfort of conversation with someone who knows me, my family, so well. Josh took his eyes off the road and snuck a glance at me.

"How's your mom? Have you talked recently?" He asked the question carefully, aware that he was treading in dangerous waters again.

"She's okay," I said, staring at the walls that separated the freeway from the housing developments. On some of them, ivy or some other green heat-loving, indestructible plant cascaded down the wall as though the botanical life could hide the ugly deadness of the blocks. "She's still in Boston at the cancer center and she stays really busy. We both do. We e-mail sometimes and she called a couple of weeks ago, but we only talked for a sec because she was in between patients. She's fine, we're both fine. It's fine."

I knew Josh wanted to say something else, I could feel it in the way his body tensed toward me, but instead he flipped his turn signal on and pulled off the freeway exit. I kind of wished he would have said what he wanted to say. I didn't get to talk to anyone about my mom and he knew. About her, about the reasons she left and the reasons she stayed away. About how lost and small I felt without a mother around to teach me things. How her being gone meant I'd had to figure things out myself for a long time.

Josh knew a lot. More than I wanted him to, maybe.

The arena was only a couple of blocks from the freeway. It was a tall, nondescript grayish building with a marquee that listed the events for the next three weeks. The UCLA Delta Gamma Charity Fashion Show was middle on the list, one week from today.

Josh pulled into the parking lot and we walked in through a side door.

A woman stood at the center of the arena and smiled at us as we approached. She had a pretty face. A face I recalled seeing around school before, somewhere.

"You must be Josh," she said, holding out her hand. "From the fraternity. Thanks for your email yesterday. I'm Olga Schwartz."

"I'm Katie Sawyer," I said as they shook hands. "President of Delta Gamma. I'll be covering for Chelsea."

A dark look crossed Olga's face, but she didn't ask why I was taking over. Had she seen the news? She looked me up and down, taking in my height and weight and outfit and probably my sign, my GPA and my fiscal worth, as well. It wasn't unusual. Girls were always scrutinized like this. Especially sorority girls. As though being social and looking nice meant we didn't have brains or hearts. That's why I worked so hard to maintain a certain image. One misstep and people brushed you aside like just another Barbie wannabe. But as quickly as her face darkened, she switched gears and smiled at both of us.

"I'm happy you're here," she said, grabbing a clipboard off the wall. "The fashion show is a good idea and the funds will be useful for our spay and neuter program."

That sounded like just the sort of thing that would make Chelsea happy. She had a soft spot for animals. Sometimes she made me help her write letters to cosmetics companies who couldn't care less about dripping soap into bunnies' eyes. I didn't mind doing that. Who would?

"Glad to hear it," I said.

Olga nodded and looked me over a moment longer then looked down at her clipboard.

"Josh, you wanted to take some measurements? I'll show you where we're setting up the stage. Katie, I brought photos of the dogs that we'll be using for the fashion show, but I left them in my car. There're in an envelope on the passenger seat. Would you mind grabbing them? It's the silver Mercedes out front. When you get back, I'll introduce you to the star of the show."

I took the keys she held out while they started working on stage stuff. The envelope was where she said it would be and I thumbed through the photos before going back in. The cutest dogs stared back at me. I couldn't wait to see them all dolled up alongside the sorority models.

When I got back into the arena, Olga held a beautiful Rottweiler on a leash.

"This is Peanut," she said. "You want to hang out with him while we talk logistics?"

"Definitely," I said. Peanut and I walked around the arena, then into the back hallways. I paused and hugged him, scratched his ears and belly, played with him. He loved it. I loved it, more.

"How could anyone give up a sweetie like you?"

"He's awesome," Josh said, coming up behind me and Peanut. He reached in, scratching Peanut under the chin. Peanut pressed his head into Josh's hand and let out a little grunt of happiness. I laughed.

"Magic hands," I said.

"You know it." Josh faced me with a laugh and I loved it: seeing his eyes crinkle at the corners, his easy smile lifting the entire mood around us. He was easy to be with, when I let down my guard.

I pressed my face into Peanut's side. "I do know it."

Josh's hands stopped. I took a slow breath and ran my fingers over Peanuts back. I meant it, how I knew about Josh's magic hands. How I remembered. I snuck a peek at him. He was staring at me, a million questions in his eyes. A million thoughts I didn't know how to respond to. Not with my words, at least. My body knew how to respond. My heart rate increased and my breathing deepened. Every sense stood at attention, waiting for his next move.

He started, as though pushed out of a daydream, and patted Peanut on the head one last time. Then he stood. "I have to finish the measurements. I just wanted to meet Peanut."

He walked away, down the hallway, and I watched him go, my skin covered with a sudden chill.

#

After half an hour, Peanut and I headed back to the open arena. I stopped in my tracks and folded my arms across my chest when I saw Josh with his back turned towards me, laughing at something Olga had said or done. From my angular vantage point I could see Olga reach her hand out and touch Josh's elbow as she laughed along with him.

I felt weird standing there watching them, and not icky weird or voyeuristic weird like I had just stumbled upon an awkwardly intimate scene, but uncomfortable weird, as though I would fly into a fit of temper and storm away from their laughter or maybe stamp my foot in a huff and demand that she take her hand off my, uh, former next door neighbor.

I cut off a sigh of irritation. So *that* explained the way she looked at me earlier.

I pulled my phone out and checked for a text from Damon. A reminder, I guess, about what was off limits. Nothing from my boyfriend.

I brushed my hair out of my eyes and walked over to them.

"Peanut's such a great dog," I said, placing my fingers on Josh's lower back and handing his leash back to Olga. Josh turned to me as though I had electrocuted him and dropped his smile. My heart leapt in a little dance of victory. So much for that off-limits reminder.

"That's why I brought him," Olga said. Then she tucked her hair behind her ear with her wedding ring displaying left hand. Typical. A flirty married lady. "But I'd love for you to meet more of the dogs. Get them used to the arena. To you."

"Sure. That would be fun. Are we done for today?" I asked. "I have to get back. I've got a few things to do this afternoon."

Olga nodded at us. "I have your emails and you have mine. Keep me up to date on developments, please. Let's meet again before the weekend. Let me know which day and I can arrange that."

Josh and I said goodbye and climbed into his car. I slumped into the passenger's seat, securing my seatbelt and staring out the window while Josh pulled out of the parking lot. The day wore on me. The whole week wore on me. I felt tired and irritable and in need of a break. Josh asked me how I liked the dogs. I said something offhand in response, though I couldn't remember what, but I didn't think it was very nice. He turned the music up, ignoring me from that point on.

And that was good. I preferred it when he was ignoring me. When we didn't have to pretend to be friends. To remember we had ever been friends. And more. We had to work together on this project, he gave me a lift to the arena. Great. It didn't have to go beyond that. Years and years of living next door to each other, years of knowing the most intimate things about each other, left behind. Our relationship, if it could be called that, was simple and uncomplicated that way.

I thought instead about Chelsea and Charlie and her cryptic e-mails and how she was gone and we would never again spend a weekend arguing which were hotter, actors or athletes. And how I didn't have anyone to take away that lonely feeling in my classes and how the only person I had been able to have a comfortable silence with for the past three and a half years was gone now and I was stuck in a car with a guy that had turned up the volume on his radio so that he could drown me out.

Who was Katie Sawyer without her BFF? Without the girl who supported her, whispered and giggled with her in the middle of science labs, spooned her when it dipped below fifty degrees at night, told me I really could do it all?

The brick walls flew by as we left the valley but it wasn't our speed that made them so blurry.

10

Sunday mornings were always reserved for brunch with Dad. It was a benefit of going to a college only a few miles away from my home in Beverly Hills. I'd never told him—maybe he just knows it because that's what dads do—but as much as I loved my DG sisters and hanging out with Damon and my classes and everything else about college life . . . I needed those mornings. A time and place to just be me. Regular, dorky Katie Sawyer. Not DG president, not girlfriend of the hottest guy on campus, not that girl who has to work extra hard to prove to the overwhelming number of men in the science programs that I belong there, too.

It all was exhausting and here, sitting on the sunny back deck, I could take a breath.

Even back when my step-mom, Alexis, was around it was just me and Dad. She was good about scheduling her hair appointments or nail appointments or affair appointments or whatever on Sunday mornings. It kept her from having to do the whole family thing that she tried so hard to avoid.

Dad liked puttering around in the kitchen, even if he had no idea what he was doing in there. He always came in with his slippers and pajamas on and flung the fridge open with verve as though he was an adventurer facing off with Mount

Everest. And then he would just stand there, the fridge door hanging open as he attempted to decipher the contents of all the neatly marked Tupperware containers that our chef Guy had stacked inside. We usually ended up with scrambled eggs and fruit and orange juice because those were the things Dad could handle.

Then we would sit out on the deck and Dad would peruse the newspaper for a few moments before attacking me with questions about school and friends and plans and things like that.

I'd raced here after the arena visit with Josh, but Dad was spending an inordinate amount of time perusing the paper. It must have been unusually fascinating news. I couldn't say I minded too much, because what was there to talk about? "Gee, how was your dead best friend's funeral?"

I sipped at my orange juice and stared out over our expansive lawns. I squinted at the fountain on the far side of the yard and took in the spring flowers. It was pretty and it was calming, sitting here with my father. Our time.

It was a surprise when the doorbell rang the moment my father picked up the business section. We looked at each other, determining who should get up and get it, a silent battle of wills. Dad unfolded the paper, gave it a snap and held it in front of his face.

"I *know* it's not for me," he said dismissively. I hid a smile and got up.

Dad was right. When I opened the door I wasn't expecting Damon to be standing on the porch, his back to the door and sunglasses on, but there he was. When I said his name he turned around and lifted his glasses to sit on top of his head. Then he grabbed me in a bear hug that left me breathless.

"I know Sundays are your whole Dad-Daughter thing," he said as he gently set me back down. "But I haven't talked to you for like two whole days and I think that you were kind of upset Friday afternoon so I thought I'd come by and see you. Hey," he said as he tipped up my face and touched my lips with his. "I worry about you."

In my head I asked him why, then, didn't he follow me from the memorial on Friday or call me even once yesterday, but I brushed those thoughts aside and let something safer come out of my mouth.

"That's sweet of you to come by." I held the door open for him. "Do you want to come in and have something to eat?"

"With your dad?" He jiggled his keys in his hand, nervously. "Can't we just go for a drive instead?" Damon gave me the dodgy "I'd rather not meet the wrong end of my girl's dad's shotgun" look.

"Stop it. You've talked to him what, a million times?" I grabbed his shirt and dragged him through the house to the backyard while he muttered about how it never got any easier no matter how many times it had been. Dad, once he realized who it was, lowered his paper and carefully refolded it along the crease. He held his hand out to Damon and they shook hands.

"Ah, Damon. Good afternoon, son. We don't usually see you here Sundays."

"Morning, sir," he replied. Damon didn't call *anyone* sir. Just my father. It was always funny to watch him cower before my dad, but my dad did that to people. To guys, at least. "I just wanted to come by and make sure Katie was all right."

Dad shot me a look and didn't look back at Damon when he said, "That's very thoughtful of you." He tossed the paper on the table and stood with his glass in hand. "I'm going to get a refill. Can I get you something to drink, Damon?"

"Sure, thanks. That would be great, sir."

I thought about returning to my chair, but I felt restless and anxious with Damon standing next to me. He breathed over my shoulder. It was heavy. And noisy.

"Let's walk," I said, as I descended the stairs to the grass and marched in the direction of the fountain. I felt and heard Damon walking behind me, moving like a bear through a thick forest, stomping his feet and brushing up against anything he possibly could brush up against. I'd never noticed before just how noisy he was.

"How was the funeral?" he asked once we'd reached the fountain and paused in our movements. He dug the toe of his shoe into the soil of the flower bed that edged the base of the fountain.

I watched the water bubble out of the top of the fountain and drop into the first bowl below the spout. Chelsea had jumped into this fountain with nothing but her underwear on last summer. It was two in the morning and we had just finished a marathon Leo DiCaprio movie session and she was feeling antsy. So she went running out to the backyard, dropping pieces of clothing one at a time across the lawn until she was in nothing but her panties (out of respect for my fountain, she told me laughingly later). Then she leaped in with a mighty splash and coaxed me in with her. If you think two hot teenagers in nothing but their underwear splashing each other in a backlit fountain is every straight, horny teenage boy's dream, you'd be right. But no one saw us that night because we weren't there to be seen. We were there to be ourselves.

"Why didn't you come?" I returned. "You were invited. I could have used you there." I sat on the edge of the fountain as Damon took his classic defensive pose: body half-turned away, hands low on his hips, staring at nothing off in the distance. I saw in him what everyone saw in him: a tall, dark and gorgeous boy with the hard body of an athlete and everything his family's mountains of money could buy. A million people told us we were perfect for each other. I guess that's why we were together. But sometimes, I saw other things.

"It's not really my thing, Katie. That thing at school was hard enough to deal with. I needed to stay away from all of it."

He thought the memorial was hard to deal with? Did he not remember the way I stumbled out of there like a suburban wife on her fifth martini before noon? But surprise would be wasted on his reaction. That was classic Damon. He made it a point to avoid the hard stuff. He brought *me* out of the hard stuff. I wouldn't have minded being let off the hook either.

"But staying away from it all meant you were staying away from me," I said, counting the koi as they swam below me. They were orange and white and speckled fish, grown to just the right size for the fountain. I bet they remembered the two mostly naked girls from last summer. "I could have used you next to me."

I could have used someone completely grounded to remind me that the things that were happening were real. To erase the surrealism of a priest in filmy white and gold against a backdrop of black. To hear the words and the music, when all I could hear was the sound of bees. To hold the hands I pressed against my thighs until my legs bruised.

"Aw, K, I don't like being used." The half-joke rolled off his tongue before he realized how angry it would make me. He rushed to sit next to me when he saw my reaction. "I'm sorry. Just kidding. I just don't do well with funerals and all that. Cut me some slack, Katie. You wouldn't want me there, all uncomfortable and shit. I'd have been useless. You probably would have been even more stressed, worried about me saying or doing the wrong thing."

I nodded as he put his hand tentatively on my shoulder. Behind him the azaleas tucked under the shadows of the fence were blooming, opening their petals to the little bit of sun that permeated that corner of the yard. Their hot pink flowers were showy against their waxy green leaves.

I would let it go. I had to let it go. This was Damon. He had nothing to hide.

"Damon, were any of the guys seeing Chelsea?"

He shrugged and I knew he didn't want to talk about anything to do with Chelsea anymore. He was studying the azaleas now, too. "Not that I knew of."

"But they might not have been talking about it? Maybe keeping it a secret?"

Damon grunted.

"No way. No one would keep a secret like that. Getting it from some way hot sorority chick? No way. The bragging rights are way too high. Especially if it was Chelsea. Everyone wanted a piece of Chelsea Mathis."

He spoke her name so wistfully that I glared at him. A thought struck me that was so wild I almost cried out. Damon wanted a piece of Chelsea? What if he'd . . . gotten it?

"Uh, except for me," he added hastily.

I let out the breath I was holding in. There was no way Chelsea would do that to me. She was my best friend. Besides, Damon wasn't her type. And Damon? How could be possibly kill someone when he barely knew how to tie his own shoes? It would take more advance planning than he could be bothered with.

But all the secrets, all the things she didn't tell me, meant every possibility would linger in my mind. Even if I thought I *knew*.

"She was pregnant."

"I heard. It's gotten around."

"So someone got her pregnant."

"That's what it sounds like."

A chill shot up my spine. He wouldn't look at me. He stared at nothing in the distance.

"You wouldn't cheat on me, would you?"

He jerked. "Wait, are we still talking about Chelsea?"

"Are we?"

I couldn't see his eyes behind his glasses, couldn't tell if it was his typical Damon confused look or something else, something calculated.

No. Not Damon. And especially not Chelsea.

Stop thinking it, Katie. You're going nuts.

But my heart raced, despite my logic. Damon was a big guy. Strong. Strong enough to overpower Chelsea.

Or me.

A sob escaped my mouth.

Damon moved to me, but I scooted away, staring at his hands.

"What is *wrong* with you?"

"Where did you get that key?"

I had that key, too. The one with the plastic red cover imprinted with a dna strand. The one Professor Griffin custom designed because, as he said, he was a little nerdy that way.

The one to the science labs.

He looked down at the ring dangling from his finger. "From Professor Conlin. She made me move some AV equipment around on Monday. For you science nerds to borrow. That's why I was by your classroom that morning."

"And you didn't give it back?"

"I only have classes with her on Monday. I haven't had the chance. What the hell—"

"You never answered my question."

"About cheating on you? God, Katie."

"God . . . what?"

He shuffled his feet. "Are you feeling guilty?"

"What?"

"I saw him."

"Him?"

His eyes raised to a point over my head. "Your old neighbor. You were talking to him in front of his frat."

I gaped at him. I didn't think he remembered that I even knew Josh, much less had a history with him. I might have mentioned Josh...once, in passing? "We're teamed up for the fundraiser. It should have been Chelsea talking to him." I forced myself to look away. Is that all this was? Me, channeling my own guilt onto Damon? I couldn't deny there was a moment, earlier, when we were playing with Peanut. A moment that, had Josh said a certain thing, made a certain move, it might have been Damon who had the right to accuse me of cheating.

A pretty scrub jay with vibrant blue and somber gray feathers and a round white belly soared in and landed on the top tier of the fountain. It jerked its head our way and considered us for a moment, then gave us a sharp *jree* and spread its wings, flying over the tennis courts and into Josh's yard. I let my eyes wander up to Josh's window, but there was no movement up there.

I looked at Damon again, searching for emotion and truth behind his sunglasses. I couldn't shake the possibility, though. Had he cheated? Had he cheated with . . . ? I clutched the bench, squeezed my eyes closed and opened them again. Crazy. Too crazy.

"You know what? You're right. I wouldn't want you to have to deal with that. The funeral thing. And I'm sorry if you felt obligated at all." I tried to keep my voice neutral, tried to keep any fear out of it that threatened to reveal my doubts. It was impossible that it could have been him. "I think I might need a little bit of time, actually, to sort this all out."

Damon nodded eagerly. He took a deep breath and changed the tone of his voice to one of affected concern.

"Yeah, you're right. Chelsea was your best friend. These things take time to deal with."

"Sure." *Deal* with? Oh, Damon. This wasn't a business proposition. "I just don't want this to be hard on you. You've already done enough. So I'm going to take a few days for myself, all right?"

Damon gave my hand a squeeze, but I balked at his touch. And then I felt like shit for not wanting it. It wasn't…magic.

"That sounds like a good idea. I'll be just a phone call away today if you need me, and I'll come get you before your class in the morning, okay? Walk you there."

I looked at Josh's window again. A shadow crossed behind the window and moved away again. Did he go home after dropping me off? I patted the top of Damon's hand. Pretend normal.

"I think I'll walk by myself tomorrow. It'll give me time to think."

Damon nodded again. Anything would be fine. Anything that brought us away from Chelsea, from my needs.

I copied his smile, pleased with how mellow it looked as my face reflected in his sunglasses.

11

I walked him to the door, leaving my hand on the knob long after I'd closed it behind him, waiting for the trembling to stop. What did he say that was so bad? Nothing. Except the part about other girls giving it up. But that was nothing new. I had nothing to fear. It was Damon. Harmless, playful Damon. I brushed my hand absently across my forehead, waiting for the churning in my stomach to subside, then went upstairs to change. First rule: breathe. Second rule: have something to do.

I came back down in my swimsuit to do a few laps when the doorbell rang again. Please, oh, please let that not be Damon back for round two. I'd just settled my whirring brain and he couldn't keep his mitts off me when I was in my bikini. I wrapped my towel around my waist and answered the door with the best Stepford Wife look I could scrounge. Ice was the only thing that froze Damon's zeal.

But it wasn't Damon who stood on my porch this time. It was Josh. And he was visibly upset. Had he cracked the identity of Sigma2992? Was it someone we knew? Was it the ex-boyfriend after all? Oh my gosh. I dropped the ice princess hauteur immediately. And I crossed my arms across my chest because I felt exposed all of a sudden but then dropped them to my side when I realized how that pressed my breasts up in my halter top.

But he noticed. The first movement and the second. He noticed and his eyebrows rose. My face filled with heat.

"What do you want, Josh?" I shot at him, deciding that the best place for my hands was on my hips.

"Do you greet everybody this way?" he snapped back.

"Nope. Just you. So what do you want?"

He stared at me and my breath came ragged. Damn those eyes. Damn wanting him so much when I know I can't.

"I have some news," he said, his voice strangely subdued now, "but I don't think you'll actually care."

News? About Sigma2992? He couldn't leave with news about that. I reached out for him and caught the back of his shirt as he turned away. I needed to rein in that attitude. I closed my eyes briefly and calmed myself.

"Okay, I'm sorry. Come in."

He stepped over the threshold and waited for his eyes to adjust to the interior darkness. We moved together into the living room where I curled up on the couch and he sat in a chair opposite me. I fiddled with my ponytail and avoided looking at him as he settled in. Did I really want to learn what he knew? Ignorance is bliss, after all.

"I just heard from Olga," he began. "The dog you were hanging out with today? Peanut? There . . . was a problem. He got sick, suddenly."

I pictured the handsome animal looking at me with a sloppy grin. I pictured his beautiful large head and his silky coat and, for some reason, before he even had to finish what he had come here to say, I knew exactly what was going to come out of Josh's mouth next and the surety of that knowledge overwhelmed me and made my body shake and closed off my throat and pounded in my brain.

I knew what he was going to tell me about that dog and I didn't really want to know, and the emotion, the emotion brought on by I dog I barely even knew, swooped in and completely overwhelmed me, and before I knew it I was the one gasping and shuddering and aching inside for this gorgeous dog that had gotten sick. That had, I knew, died suddenly.

Josh leaped the coffee table and came in next to me and gathered me up as I fell because of this thing, this teeny tiny little thing that I couldn't control.

"Hey, K, I'm sorry," Josh whispered, rubbing my back. And his hand felt so good there, and his words and his voice were so right that it brought on another wave of feeling.

"What happened?" I choked out between dry heaves. He was going to be my dog, the one I'd strut down the catwalk with. Everything I touched died. Peanut and Chelsea. My parents' marriage. Simon.

"A seizure. Probably from a stroke. Olga didn't know yet." Josh stroked, stroked, stroked. And I could have sat there forever with him doing that. Except that I couldn't. I just couldn't let that happen.

Count, Katie, count. One, two, three, four, five, six, seven, eight, nine, ten. Yes, there was a center in there, in me, somewhere. It was hiding better and better each day, but it was there. Abruptly, I pulled away from Josh and sat up, back straight and brushed at my eyes angrily with the edge of my towel.

Breathe, Katie, breathe. I took the air in through my nose, focused on keeping it steady and smooth, let it out through my mouth. I repeated the motion again and again until I very nearly forgot that Josh was even there.

"Katie?" he asked. And now he was the one confused.

I turned back to him. He sat sunk back into the couch, the place where I had been still dictating the curve of his back, his arms. I gazed at him, wanting for it to be okay. But it wasn't. I couldn't let these things get to me. And I couldn't let Josh be the one to pick me up again.

He'd hurt me before, back when he'd said things would be okay after Simon and my mom, but they weren't ever okay and I blamed him for that—for saying it would all work out when it didn't. So I'd made him hurt when I called him a liar, when I told him to stay out of my life.

Maybe . . . I'd regretted that. Before. But not now. I should be past all of that. I know I should. But . . . I just wasn't. Because I'd never let myself deal with it. I didn't have time to take off from school for a break, I didn't have the capacity to let my emotions take over when I was too busy taking care of Dad, and then my DG sisters. And Josh . . . he was better off like this. He didn't need to get pulled down with me and I certainly didn't need him telling me everything was going to be okay. I couldn't do that again. Let him be my rock, let my heart belong to him, let his fingers leave streaks of desire like burn marks across my skin the way only he could. And then lose it all.

Those people we used to be? That was a lifetime ago. I moved on. Spent my time struggling to stay afloat, to be the girl everyone expected me to be. That I expected me to be.

"I'm fine," I said, my voice calm and collected once more. I tucked a stray hair behind my ear and fixed my towel as best as I could without having to stand. "Thanks for bringing that news. It couldn't have been easy."

He sat forward and stared at me as though I was the earthly incarnation of insanity.

"Olga wanted to tell you herself, actually, to say thanks for your help."

"Oh," I said. "Did you give her my number?"

He made a noise, doubtful and scornful.

"Are you kidding? Not when you react like this to things."

His comment stung like a slap to the side of the face. But I raised my chin in the air, because this was what I was good at: taking everything in stride. Being the one everyone else could count on.

"React like what, exactly?"

"Like this," he said. "Like this ball of unrestrained emotion that just takes over you for, like, two seconds before you flip a switch and turn it off suddenly. It's scary and you've got to stop it or it's only going to get worse. It's just like when—"

"Is that all you had to tell me?"

He stared at me again, and this time I knew he was pissed. I could see it in the flash of his eyes and the stiffness that radiated off his entire body. He stood and walked towards the foyer before stopping and turning back to me.

"You've got to stop being like this, Katie. It's not helping."

I stood, too, clutching at my towel as it fell from my hips.

"You're not helping, either, Josh." I crammed as much venom into my words as I could without actually spitting them out. More than four years I'd kept him at bay. I wouldn't let my streak die now. "Go home."

He glared at me then threw his hands in the air, palms forward, like he always did when I was beating him down and he'd had enough. Then he left.

I closed my eyes. I knew—and it scared me more than I wanted it to—that someday he would stop coming back. For good.

#

"Who is that guy in the house next door?"

I'd finished my twentieth lap, felt my hands touch the wall of the pool, and pulled myself out to sit on the side. Water pooled around me. Chelsea used to come over, swim with me. Question me.

"That's a cute bikini," I replied, avoiding her question.

She stuck her bust out and twisted back and forth for me. The red frills on her top danced with the movement. So did her hair.

"Thanks," she said. "I've always had a great body for wearing almost nothing."

I laughed with her and we splashed our feet in and out of the water, higher and higher until we had to move to the side to dodge the water. The sun made a line in the pool that ribboned like a high frequency airwave as we moved. She waited patiently for me to answer her question, but I wasn't sure if I wanted to.

"His name is Josh," I'd finally said.

"Josh. And that's all you're going to tell me? Totally hot literal boy next door and all I get is a name."

"Yes."

"Kaaaaaatie."

"It's complicated," I'd told her. She'd heaved a gargantuan sigh next to me.

"It always is with you," she'd said, *"but it doesn't have to be. Were you two close?"*

"Does it matter? It was a long time ago. Look, I have an image to uphold. I've got to keep cool for all my peers. Be a scientist, push emotion to the sides. You know what it's like."

"Cool for all your peers? Geez, K. I mean, maybe. But nobody made you be that way. You did that to yourself."

She'd put her hand over mine as a gesture of unity.

"Katie, we're besties. But you don't make it easy to come to you with things. Not that you've ever treated anyone poorly or anything like that, but it's intimidating. To approach you with imperfections when you are so hell bent on making sure everything is perfect. Making sure you're perfect."

I'd closed my eyes against her admonition.

But now I wonder . . . had I been more approachable, would Chelsea have told me all her secrets? Would I be able to obliterate the horrible thought that my own boyfriend could be a murderer? There had always been a little bit of jealousy between them. Not on Chelsea's part, but on his. An awareness of the way I kept him at bay but let Chelsea in. Things had never been terrible between me and Damon, but I wasn't sure I'd always been fair to him.

12

I had to be back at Delta Gamma by six for our fashion show planning meeting. The designers were coming by for fittings, we had to match girls to dogs, and the non-model jobs had to be assigned. When I walked through the front door, the mood was grim.

"Was your weekend okay?" Carolina asked. The girls sprawled around the living room, watching me expectantly. I pulled myself up tall and blasted them all with a bright smile. It was my job to keep spirits high.

"It was nice seeing my Dad," I said. I pulled my planning binder from my bag and took a seat. "Are we ready to begin?"

Carolina and Stacey gave each other a look.

"You missed a lot today," Stacey said. She paused and I knew she wouldn't go on until I responded.

"What did I miss?" I asked.

Stacey puckered her lips and milked the moment. She crunched a cucumber between her teeth. I locked eyes with junior Courtney Dreger, our resident reluctant sorority sister. Her band, Ladies in Waiting, were providing the music for the fashion show. Normally, I could count on her to be tough in any situation, but after a moment, her eyes filled with tears and she looked away.

Stacey crossed the room and flopped down next to me.

"Big news. A janitor was arrested. Like, an hour ago. It happened right outside my English class, where I just happened to be waiting for Sergio to drop off the assignment I had forgotten. The cops came in, four of them. Knocked on his office door. When he answered they slapped their cuffs on him and read him his rights. Right in the middle of the hallway."

"Why was your pool boy bringing you your English homework? Are you guys screwing around again?"

Stacey paused her chewing and glared at me.

"Okay, fine. Why did they arrest the janitor? What did they find out?"

Stacey finished her cucumber and sucked on her teeth.

"Well, word is that the night before Chelsea was found? Professor Lee was in the classroom right across from the chem lab and she heard this rolling sound in the hallway, then some other sounds like the janitor struggling with something heavy. So, then it went quiet and she heard the rolling sound again, headed back the way it came."

I shook my head, tasting acid in my mouth. "That's not much to go on."

Stacey continued. "Then the police found a photo of the National Science finals, the one you and Chelsea placed at, taped up in his janitor's closet. And it was signed by Chelsea. Oh my gosh you guys, I was there when he asked her to sign it! Right in the middle of the hallway he just stopped her and asked her for her autograph. And she gave it to him! Right there! When they arrested him I pulled one of the officers aside to tell him that I was there when Chelsea signed the picture. He said thanks—he was kind of cute!—and then he started talking with another cop about how they had found a ticket to Guatemala or somewhere like that at his house and they thought he was a flight risk. Crazy stuff."

"So they arrested him because he probably had plans to visit his family one of these days and because he had a crush on Chelsea?"

"Duh, I mean, the guy was, like, forty. Gross. Don't you find that a little odd?"

Actually, I didn't.

"Besides, that isn't even the biggest piece of evidence. My cousin's friend, you know the one who reports for channel five? He found out that they took the janitor's clothes in for testing and they found DNA on his shirt. And not just any DNA. Chelsea's! You can't deny the DNA, ladies."

"But she wasn't bleeding," Carolina choked out.

Stacey rolled her eyes and broke off a piece of dried mango.

"Maybe she spit on him. Or maybe it was . . . something else. Something I totally don't want to think about. You know what I mean."

I tried not to choke on *my* own spit.

"What was his name?" I said. Stacey returned my question with an unbelievable look.

"What was his name? What the hell do I care what some crazy serial killer freak's name was? Didn't you just hear me? He rolled his cart down the hall, paused to kill Chelsea and stuff her in the closet, then rolled it away and went back to work. Does it get any sicker than that? He's a freaking freak that deserves to get the electric chair. That guy was around us all the time. He could have been planning this for ages. Geez, Katie. I thought you'd be a little more riled up than this."

"Yeah," I muttered, "I should be. I should be . . . glad. They found the killer." But I wasn't. I couldn't feel much of anything. I knew I needed to apologize to Damon. For suspecting. But I was realizing that the hunt for the killer was something to keep me occupied, something to take my mind off the fact that I was going to have to grieve at some point. Accept that Chelsea was, in fact, gone.

And I didn't want to do that. I wasn't strong enough.

Stacey rested her head on my shoulder. "Well, I'll say it even if no one else will. I finally feel safe again. I've spent the whole week thinking someone was going to break in and murder us all in our beds or something."

Stacey was right. We were safe. But all I could wonder was how and where did he drown her near the chem labs that would be emptied of witnesses? I shook my head. I was questioning everything, lately. A good avoidance strategy. But Chelsea was . . . dead.

I started as Carolina touched my shoulder from behind the couch. Her eyes were fixed on me, brimming with tears. I took her hand in mine and squeezed. She responded with a subdued, but relieved, breath.

"Anyway, that's not all," Stacey went on. "Professor Griffin is gone."

I scanned the living room as though Professor Griffin would pop out and debunk Stacey's claim.

"Where did he go?" I asked.

"Took personal leave," Stacey said. "Not that I can blame him. I'd be pretty shaken up if one of my students' bodies fell out of my closet. And all the suspicion? The police hanging around and everything. And I've heard a million people say he's the one who did it. Like he could. But it's got to take a toll."

"Some of us could use personal leave," Carolina said.

Stacey nodded, but with her news divulged, she went back to her list of designers and shut up.

My mind kept working. And I knew it was just something to do, that my thoughts needed to stop, but dealing with loss, with someone leaving *me*, was so, so hard.

"But he could have," I blurted. "He's really flirty. What if," I pressed on, my eyes closed just for a second, "what if they were . . . together and he . . . "

"I don't know, K," Carolina said. "He's a professor."

"Every professor sleeps with students," Stacey said.

Carolina wrinkled her nose. "Yeah, but . . . "

"But what?" I said. "Aren't people always saying they never thought the killer seemed like the type?"

"Griffin could get any girl he wanted," Stacey said. "What would he be doing with an undergrad? Especially a poor one?"

"Jealous much?"

"Whatever, Katie. You haven't proven anything. He has a tiny salary. If he was going to go after one of us, it would be one with money."

"You think that's all that matters?"

"Please don't start dishing relationship advice."

"Excuse me?"

"Everyone else sees how you and Damon are so perfect for each other except me."

"You're imagining things," I said, imbuing my voice with the nonchalantness required to send Stacey off the scent. The last thing I needed was for her to start buzzing about how platinum couple Katie Sawyer and Damon Brinkley were taking a break so that Katie could regain her sanity.

The doorbell rang and I jumped up, grateful to escape Stacey.

"Sorry I'm late." Josh stood on the porch, decked out in a sweaty t-shirt, shorts and soccer cleats. I wanted to wrinkle my nose at his get-up, but I stumbled, my eyes drawn to his legs. His well-muscled, soccer playing legs. He lifted his shirt to wipe his face, flashing his abs and I clutched the door harder. Maybe I was losing my sanity. And I wanted to find it again down Josh's pants.

"What are you doing here?"

"Carolina told me to come by for the planning meeting. I just got done with practice, but I came as quickly as I could."

"Obviously." I held the door open wider, fumbling for something to say that would erase the image of his lean stomach in my head. "You stink. But come in. The designers will be here soon. There's a bathroom down the hall you can clean up in. Then you can start doing that 'helping' thing you're so good at."

He frowned and hesitated in the doorway. I bit the inside of my mouth. Why did I always do this, say these things, to Josh? One more wrong word from me and he would leave. Is that what I really wanted him to do? I didn't know. But reminding myself that he was here for the dogs, not for me, helped dissipate my confusion, if not my desire. I cleared my throat. Tried to make my voice crisp and professional. But it came out soft, anyway.

"Thank you for coming. We really appreciate your help on this project."

Josh ran a hand over the back of his neck and sighed, but he came in, finally. After he sort of cleaned up, boy-style, we got down to business. The designers came and fitted the girls with their outfits, we created a board with their photos and the dogs', and Josh detailed Triangle's plans for the catwalk.

"This is really good," I said, looking at his notes over his shoulder. He was so talented. I loved his brains. I loved . . .

I needed to not be sitting next to him.

"Thanks." He grinned. The past half hour working together had cleared the air between us. Things, *everything*, felt good in a way they hadn't for a long time. It seemed that we both noticed the change. "This whole project has been fun. Creative, but in a different way than I usually work with. It was a really good idea."

"It was Chelsea's idea," I said, softly. I knew I'd told him that, already. I cleared my throat and pointed to his sketch. "What if we added pretend hydrants right there. How fun would that be?"

"Totally." He brought his pencil across the paper to where my hand was, ready to draw the hydrants in. Our fingers touched, shooting a little *zing* up my arm. I reluctantly pulled away. His pencil hesitated as he glanced at me. I met his eyes. Offered a small smile. God, it felt good doing this project with him. He was so easy to be with. He nudged me in the shoulder and my smile turned into a laugh.

"Hey, we should meet more of the dogs soon."

He nodded. "I'll call Olga. Maybe tomorrow?"

"I can make time."

"Good. I'll even let you take over the music. Your taste is . . . okay," he teased. I nudged him back and he chuckled. "Listening to anything new, lately?"

"Yeah. There's this one band—"

My words were cut off by the doorbell ringing again.

"It's for Katie," Courtney Dreger called over her shoulder.

I caught Josh's eye as Damon walked in. Put more space between us. Tucked my hair behind my ears.

"Hey." Damon smiled as he reached in for a kiss. I turned my head so he caught my cheek instead of my lips. Next to me, Josh got to his feet and started gathering his things.

"What are you doing here?" I said. My body buzzed with tension. These two guys didn't belong in the same room at the same time.

Josh nodded at Damon. "Hey."

"How's it going?" Damon said. His eyes were guarded, as though he could sense the strain. He was usually oblivious to that sort of thing. "Just checking in on my girl. We're taking some time, you know. Katie here needs some time. She's been through a ton of shit lately."

"Thanks for announcing that," I said.

"What? Everyone knows it's true. There's no need to hide it. Just let it out, you know?"

I stepped back from Damon's fingers, sweeping over my thighs. His touch felt wrong, gave me shivers, but not the good kind. Josh looked away, his face shadowed.

"I've got to run," Josh said. "I have to be up early for a game tomorrow. I think we've got everything good to go."

"Oh yeah, is that the Spring Carnival thing? That's my girl. Keeping busy. Keeping your mind off Chelsea. Those are the kinds of things that heal, you know?" He nodded sagely at me, but narrowed his eyes at Josh.

I stared at him, unable to stand her name being formed on anyone's lips. Speaking of her sullied her memory. Damon looked back at me hopefully, as though if I just did this one thing, I would be saved, I would be healed. Then we could go back to being normal us again. I didn't know how to tell him that I wasn't sure that I wanted to go back to normal us. That I thought I might have outgrown what we were. That janitor or no, I still wondered.

"Sure, those are the things that heal."

I looked away from Damon, ready to remind Josh about going to meet more of the dogs tomorrow. But all I saw was Josh slipping out the door without a goodbye.

13

He'd said he had an early soccer game, so I headed to the fields before my classes. His intramural team had enough of a crowd that I could slip in unnoticed to watch the last ten minutes. There was something exhilarating about watching him streak across the field, about seeing his intense expression as he passed the ball, watching his team jump all over each other when they scored.

At the way his muscles tensed and relaxed, the way he was completely zoned into the action. Passion, of a sort. I pressed my fingers to my throat. I knew that look so well. Remembered how it had been focused on me, long ago.

At the final whistle, I caught up with him on the sidelines.

"Josh, can I have a minute?"

He looked at me over his water bottle. I had just finished studying the lines of his neck and shoulders as his head tipped back for a drink. A couple other guys exchanged a look but Josh shrugged coolly and dropped his bottle in his bag.

"See you guys later," he told them. He shouldered his backpack and stood with an exaggerated sigh. "Where to?"

"We can walk, if you don't mind."

"All right."

I led him blindly away from the field. I wasn't sure where to go. I wasn't entirely sure what I wanted from Josh.

He could tell.

"Here," he said, stopping me with a touch of his finger on my arm. "Come down here. I need to drop these cones in the equipment room."

In the equipment room, dust swirled through the limited oxygen supply and the smell of sweat soaked leather dominated everything else. I plugged my nose and gave Josh a look.

"This was the only place you could think of?"

He leaned against a steel frame rack of football helmets.

"You're the one who needed alone time. Damon not meeting your needs anymore?"

I hated how we flip-flopped. How one moment with him could be absolute perfection, and the next a battle. Josh had no right to act jealous. We were nothing to each other. No matter how he made me feel. And the way he made me feel . . . frustrated me. I picked up a plastic orange cone and launched it. He ducked with an exasperating laugh.

"Shut up, Josh. When's the last time you had a girlfriend?"

It wasn't as though I expected him to list them off. We both knew he wasn't lonely. But he shrugged the question off, folding his arms across his chest, refusing to answer. His eyes, usually so warm and inviting, were closed to me.

"What do you want, Katie?"

I retrieved the cone, being sure to avoid Josh's personal space, and replaced it at the top of its stack. I straightened a shoulder pad on the shelf behind me, realized what I was touching, and wiped my hand on my skirt. Ew.

"I thought we were going to see more dogs today."

Josh looked away and I knew, immediately, that he hadn't scheduled anything with Olga last night. That shouldn't matter. We didn't need to meet the dogs. No, it didn't matter. Except . . . I had to bite the inside of my mouth to keep my lip from trembling. I cleared my throat and changed direction. "Did you find anything yet? About Chelsea's—about the frat guy?"

"You mean anything in the very short span of time between yesterday afternoon and now? What did you expect from me?"

"I'm so sorry to expect anything from you."

"Believe me, I already know that."

A heavy silence hung between us.

"Why aren't you over that, anyway?" he continued. "They arrested the janitor, didn't you hear?"

I picked a stopwatch up off one of the shelves and played with the buttons, resetting the time to zero. I set it back down quickly, hoping no one was saving that time for something important.

"Yeah, but I'm just not sure—"

"Just not sure what?"

When I failed to answer him he heaved a sigh.

"What do you want from me, Katie?"

I blinked back a surprise rush of tears. How could I tell him I wanted both everything—and nothing—from him, but that I knew I deserved less than either?

"I want to find . . . I want to know who . . ." I shook my head. Why was Josh the hardest person on the planet to talk to, when I knew for a fact he was the easiest person to talk to?

"It's not your job to solve this crime," he said, after the silence between us filled the room, pressing against our skin painfully. "You need to give your energy to dealing with it in other ways."

"Chelsea's murder," I corrected. "Not just some random crime. I don't think the janitor did it."

"Stop it," he whispered. He started to reach a hand out to me, but pulled back before touching me. I couldn't tell him that I wanted him to. To reach out to me. To touch me. To *everything*.

"I can't. Please." I'd lowered myself to whimpering. My shame had no end when it came to Chelsea.

"I don't have anything for you."

For a moment, my heart melted under the regret in his voice. But then I realized I was doing it again: setting him up to get hurt. I replaced my guilt with anger.

"Then why did you bring me in here?"

"What? I'm not the one who dragged me into this equipment closet."

I smirked. I had him there.

"Actually, yes you did."

"Right. The idea to be alone with you was mine."

I bit back my retort and paused. Wait. He didn't want to be alone with me? Was I the only one with a little belly-flutter as a result of our close quarters? I tipped my chin town and clenched my jaw. He didn't want me. He couldn't possibly want me. Not after the way I'd treated him.

I looked up again, trying to bite back my anger. It wasn't his fault that he didn't want me. "I just wanted to ask you about the username. Somewhere where your entire soccer team wasn't going to overhear. You were the one dragging us into rooms that reek of the gladiators time forgot."

He pushed off the rack and came within a foot of my face. Electricity fizzed in the air. I clutched the rack behind my back to keep from curving my body into his. Maybe, I just didn't know what anyone wanted, anymore. Including me.

"So, you're saying you don't want to be alone with me? Katie Sawyer, you break my heart."

His mouth hesitated around the next word, the one he didn't say but that we both knew had almost spilled out: *again*.

I took a shallow breath and held it, searching his face. He didn't bother hiding anything: the hurt I left him with years ago, the desire he had right now. We both knew we wanted to be here, locked away in this steamy room together, ready to test our memories of each other's bodies. I licked my lips and his eyelids drooped seductively. Another shallow breath, another beat of time. My heart thrummed in my ears. Then my hand slid across the rack and knocked three helmets to the ground. The sound they made was deafening, clinking and bouncing on the cement floor. I gasped, startled, and Josh took a step away.

"Smooth, Sawyer."

I pushed him, and he tumbled back with a hearty laugh.

"Bite me, Josh. I only came in here because I asked for a favor and I'm just checking up on it. Someone's got to keep you in line."

"Thanks, but I don't need a nanny."

"Could have fooled me."

We faced off in the equipment room while the smells of grass stains and dirty socks drifted between us.

"Are we done here?"

"Just to clarify, you haven't found out anything?"

"No, Katie, I haven't found out anything. But I'll contact your personal secretary when I do."

#

The janitor's office wasn't on my radar, so I searched the halls for it. It wasn't difficult to find. I followed an officer coming in off of lunch, tracked him across the esplanade and into one of the humanities buildings.

There was the yellow tape.

I slowed my step as I approached the officers and the room they were packing up. The detective—Red—wasn't here. It was quiet, except for the voices of the cops as they talked about their kids, the sports teams they followed, what happened on their last shifts, and the sound of items dropping into cardboard boxes. I stopped once I could see into the office, through the open door tagged by a police barrier.

I expected more. More than a chipped brown desk and a whiteboard with a map of the school hanging from a Visit Santa Cruz magnet on the wall. More than a couple of mismatched notepads and pencils on the desk. More than a bare tile floor.

Blood, maybe. Or the stench of evil. But it only smelled like bleach.

"You don't look like a detective." An officer, not the one I followed, pointed his coffee cup at me.

"I'm the Delta Gamma president," I said, as if that would explain everything.

"And? Unless you've got some pom poms in that bag of yours, I think you're in the wrong place." They laughed. Three of them. The one collecting evidence and the two on break. The fourth sipped at her coffee with a look of distaste. I edged toward her.

"Why the janitor? What makes you so sure? It could have been anyone."

Snarky Nancy Drew comments drifted my way.

"Did you know the girl?"

I nodded. "And it doesn't make sense. I think . . . the janitor was harmless." I bit my lip. They didn't want to know what I thought. I hardly knew what I thought. Why should I care about defending a stranger? Surely these cops knew what they were doing.

"Maybe he wasn't so harmless," the female cop said. "People aren't always what they seem."

"You're sure it wasn't Professor Griffin? She fell out of his closet, you know."

"Do you know something about him that could help us?"

I knew things. Lots of things. But not the right kinds of things. I probably shouldn't even have said that. Stacey was right. No way it was Griffin. I shook my head.

The officer took another sip of her coffee. "I wish I could help you get through this, but I'm not authorized to talk about the investigation. If you have any information, you should go down to the precinct." She passed me a business card, but I'd seen that one before and I didn't really know anything, anyway. Josh was right. I needed something to occupy my thoughts. To take up space. "I'm sorry about your friend. We're doing everything we can."

"But she was—"

"Katie?"

I looked up at the sound of my name and a rumbling of wheels on bare floor.

"Olga. What are you doing here?" The vet, half-hidden behind a tall TV cart loaded with cables and video equipment approached the janitor's office.

"Returning some AV equipment I'd borrowed a long time ago. It's been sitting in the classroom for weeks. I'm bad at getting things back in time. I always have huge library fees." She stashed her overburdened ring of keys in her purse and looked to the officers for approval of her humor. One rewarded her with a companionable nod.

"She's a sorority president," a cop snarked. Olga gave me a quizzical look.

"I mean . . . what are you doing on campus?"

"I'm an adjunct for Evolutionary Biology."

"Oh." That's probably why I'd seen her before. Why Griffin knew her. "I should go."

The female cop threw me a sympathetic look as I stepped forward and looked into the office one last time. I thought there would be something more. The picture, maybe. The one she'd signed. There was nothing.

#

Josh bumped into me in the hall. On purpose. I know it was on purpose.

"Hey!"

But then he slipped something into my hand and gave me a look as he strode past, and I shut up. I unfolded the note.

Scrawled across the center in his rushed handwriting was a name.

A name and an address.

Bryant Carter. A brother in USC's Sigma Chi fraternity.

I reached for the wall, kept reaching because it felt like it was moving away from me, like it was a mirage. Grasped something. Steadied myself, breathed. Sought Josh's eyes. He leaned against a door at the end of the hallway, watching my actions. And then he was next to me, his hand on my elbow.

"It's not a perfect match. The year's wrong, but his birthday is February ninth. The ninety-two at the end might mean something else. It's a start."

I reached into my bag and fumbled for my cell. The ringer sounded the moment I flipped it open.

Charlie.

"I was just about to call you," I answered, cringing at the way my voice shook.

"There's news," Charlie replied.

I swallowed and looked at Josh again, as though I could ground my faltering emotions in his surety. But no. No. I had to breathe. Gather my own strength. Center. I closed my eyes and straightened my spine.

"What news?"

"They arrested the janitor yesterday."

"Oh. I know. I mean, I heard."

"You did?"

"Yeah."

"Do you think . . .?"

"I don't know. I can't—I don't know."

"I mean, why?"

"They say he had a crush. But, really?"

"That's what I was thinking."

"But the DNA."

"I know."

I felt the paper, Josh's note, clenched in my fist.

"Did you ever see him? What was he like?"

"Not really? I guess he was just this old, quiet guy. I'd never peg him for the mur—for that type."

"You can never tell with people. What dark secrets they're hiding."

"I guess. But, Charlie? The guy wasn't very big. How could he overpower Chelsea? She was so strong."

"I don't know. She was sick, right? Maybe worn down?"

"Maybe. But then he had to get her to the—"

"Oh, God. I don't want to think about that."

Me neither. But none of it sounded right to me. Why would some old guy just up and kill her? Had she done something mean to him? Impossible. More likely a manic breakdown from cleaning up after sloppy students day in and day out.

"Katie?"

"Hmm?"

"You said you were going to call me. You okay?"

The note.

"Oh. I have news, too. I think. Josh found someone."

"Josh?"

I swallowed. There were so many ways I could describe Josh to Charlie. But things were already getting too complicated, so I cleared my throat and forced my voice to sound as casual as possible. "The guy I was telling you about?

Who could help us? He found this guy. Bryant Carter. He's a Sigma Chi at USC. His birthday's February ninth."

"He's a match?"

"Mostly. He wasn't born in ninety-two, though."

"But that could mean something else."

"It could."

"Should we go to the cops?"

I thought about the cops and their snarky comments and frowned. I spent so much time trying to make people take me seriously.

"Maybe we could check him out first. See if he's, um, the type?"

I saw Josh next to me, shaking his head slowly at my idea and spun around so my back was to him. He sighed and his disapproval made me hesitate. But I pushed forward. I had to do this, check out Bryant Carter. For Chelsea, but also for me. So I could stop feeling like the walls of my life were shuddering at the edges, just waiting to cave in on me if I didn't find something to do.

"I know someone who does work study in the registration office there. We met at a . . . bathhouse. Maybe I can find out when his classes are."

"Okay. Call me when you know something. I'm free all afternoon." I tossed the phone back in my bag.

Josh hadn't magically disappeared when I turned back around like I'd hoped.

"What?"

"What are you doing?"

"None of your business."

"It is my business. You made me find the guy. Now I'm supposed to sit back while you let Charlie hunt him down and, what? Taser him when he's not looking? Take away his beer until he answers your questions?"

"If it comes to that, yes."

"You can't just—"

I silenced him with a raised eyebrow. We were past the time when Josh and I monitored each other. Beyond caring if we got in trouble or needing someone to watch each other's backs.

"Yeah, I can," I said. He turned on his heel and slammed his palm into a wall before walking away.

#

My last class of the day was winding down when I heard the telltale buzz. My phone flashed at me from my bag.

Engineering at 5:00. Vivian Hall. Meet in front at 4:30?

I checked to make sure no one was looking before replying.

Will be there.

I ran from the classroom, leaving my work half finished. The parking lot at Delta Gamma wasn't as empty as it should have been.

I'm not sure why he was standing there, hands on my hood as though he owned it. Looking right, perfect, waiting for me. I felt a tang of longing, of wanting him to always be waiting for me when I got out of class, finished a lesson, came home. But it had been a long time since I came home to that place, that wonderful and secret place between our houses. Where children grew up together, and then fell for each other. And there could never be a going back there. Nor was there any way he could have known about the message, now.

I tucked a hair behind my ear. "Get off my Mini."

"You should call the police."

"I tried that already."

"USC's a big place. I don't know what you think's going to happen. Stroll around campus until you find a guy that looks right?"

"Nope. We're going to catch him on his way into his five o'clock class."

I couldn't hold back the smug smile that stretched over my face as the one on Josh's fell.

"You found him?"

"Charlie did. Now get off my Mini."

But he didn't budge. "Just unlock the door. I'm not letting you go by yourself."

"I don't need your permission, Josh."

"You want to hit up a sketchy part of town alone?"

He had a point.

"Fine. But don't be a backseat driver. Or a passenger seat driver. Or whatever."

I had to admit that it was nice having him in the car. He didn't mess with my stereo like some would and he knew exactly where to find the north information booth. And he was so helpful, unfolding and studying the campus map and pointing me in the right direction. But every time he looked at me and opened his mouth like he had something to say about what we were doing, I shot him a look that said I would dump him on the side of the road if he did.

"Where are we headed?" I asked, once I'd pulled into a parking space in the garage and cut the engine.

"Actually, we're really close to Vivian. Five minutes, maybe."

"Good. I don't want to put too many miles on my new shoes."

Josh craned his neck around and glanced at my feet.

"You wore high heels to a stakeout?"

"No, I wore heels to school. The stakeout just happened."

"Don't you have other shoes in your trunk or something?"

"Uh! With this outfit? No way."

"You're insane."

"Whatever."

We exited the parking garage and hiked a couple of blocks east until we hit a plaza. I didn't know how we were going to find Charlie amongst the milling students, but he made it easy by spotting us first.

"Katie." He enveloped me in a hug. "Is this our sleuth?"

"Charlie, Josh. Josh, Charlie."

"Nice to meet you. I've already checked out the classroom. It's on the second floor. I figure we could ask one of the girls in the class which one is Bryant and go from there. Sound good?"

Josh and I nodded and followed Charlie upstairs. He stopped in front of a closed door and waited. Before long, a student joined us in the hall. Then another one and another. Any one of them could be Bryant. I took an involuntary step towards Josh as I studied them, looking for signs of lunacy.

They all had them, really. Typical engineering students.

My palms began to sweat, clenched in tight fists. I wanted, so badly, for Bryant to show up, to reek of evil, to be the solution. But if he was the one—the killer—everything Chelsea would be over. Case closed on my best friend. And even though part of me wanted to be able to move on, another part wanted to stubbornly hold on. Not admit that she was, really, gone.

I spun in a circle, as though looking for our culprit, when really I just needed to move. Josh watched me, and when his eyes ensnared mine, I lost my focus, my breath, for just a moment. I faltered, heart still. He steadied me with a finger to my hip. I tore my gaze away, that place with his fingerprint tingling.

There were a dozen guys loitering when the classroom door opened and the previous class pushed its way out. Then the hall emptied as those waiting went in. In the next five minutes, another twenty guys passed us by and entered the classroom. Five o'clock hit and the door was shut by an unseen force.

There were no girls.

"No," I breathed. "This is a travesty. Where are all the girls in science at USC?" Josh and Charlie gave each other blank looks and I sighed. "What's the name of your friend in registration?"

"Isaac Goldberg. Why?"

I opened the classroom door and popped my head in.

"Sorry to interrupt," I announced as thirty-odd faces turned to me. "But Bryant Carter is wanted in registration."

"Huh?"

Got him. Second row back, all the way over. The scrawny one. Zitty. Ew.

I scuttled backwards as the professor bore down on me with blazing eyes and a beard he could have used as a weapon.

"Uh, Isaac Goldberg wants him when class is over." I ducked out, letting the door slam behind me, and darted down the hallway, Josh and Charlie close on my heels.

"What was that?" Josh hollered as we burst into the plaza, grabbing my arm and spinning me close.

"Hey, I know who he is now."

"He could be a murderer!"

"That's why I did it!"

"But now he knows what you look like. That someone's looking for him."

"I don't care—not if he killed Chelsea!"

"I care!" Josh roared. His face was close enough to mine that I could see his pupils dilating with his rage. My hands curled into fists and my heart galloped like a wild horse set free.

"I never asked you to—"

"Isaac better not get in trouble," Charlie broke in carefully, putting a hand on Josh's shoulder and pulling him back from me. Josh ran his hand through his hair, gathering control of himself. I folded my arms and glared at them both, but it was almost hard to be angry. Not after what Josh said about caring. Did he . . . still? More importantly, did it matter? All our years apart had been a good thing. And now I was letting him get too close again. I felt pulled in two directions: what my mind knew was good for me and what, I was beginning to realize, my heart wanted.

I sighed and addressed Charlie. "He'll be fine. I know he will. Registration probably won't even be open."

"Yeah well . . . I guess at least we know which one's Bryant."

I ignored Josh's low sound of disbelief and Charlie went to get a coffee—to settle his nerves, he said—while Josh and I sat against the bricks, sucking in humid spring air, and waiting for the class to end.

He broke our fuming silence. "That wasn't cool."

"I thought it was brilliant. More than the two of you superbrains could come up with."

"He could be dangerous."

"He should be afraid of me, not the other way around."

Josh leaned his head against the bricks with a god-help-me look directed to the sky.

Five minutes passed. I studied my nail polish and tried to ignore the way my bones and muscles and skin wanted to move closer to Josh, as though he was a magnetic force I couldn't resist.

"It's quiet," I finally said, hoping conversation would dash away the need buzzing in my body.

"Not a lot of classes in the evenings."

"Do you think this guy did it?"

"I don't know him. It's possible."

"No, I mean—"

I meant, did you think this guy, anyone, could have killed Chelsea? Did you really think she was dead? Did you think it was possible, really possible, to kill a girl like her, wipe her from the planet forever?

Josh turned to me with a patient look, his eyebrows knotted with concern.

"Don't look at me like that," I whispered, huskily.

"Like what?"

"Like you expect me to bare my soul to you. Would it make you happy if I cried? Bet you'd love that."

"It wouldn't make me happy." He looked up again, counting the fluffy white clouds. "But, have you?"

"Cried?" I choked on the word. I would right now, in the middle of this stakeout, if he didn't stop asking that question. If I didn't say something to make him stop . . . being Josh. "Geez, Josh. Get all personal. Want to sniff my panties, too?"

He got up and walked away, but I stood before he got out of earshot.

"Stop making me say those kinds of things to you," I screamed. I bit my lip hard to keep the rising sobs at bay.

He checked his watch before disappearing behind another building. I sat. Caught my racing heartbeat. That was better. No more demands, no more breathing down my neck.

"Here." Charlie handed me a bottle of water when he returned.

"Thanks." I twisted the cap and took a sip. It was cold. I was cold.

"Where's Josh?"

I shrugged. "Went to find a bathroom."

Charlie eyed me closely. I squirmed under his scrutiny. "What?"

"You two."

"Us two?"

"You don't treat him very well, do you?"

"It's complicated."

"The Katie catchphrase."

"It is."

"So uncomplicate it."

"Right, it's that easy."

"Love's not always easy."

I paused, water bottle held to my lips. Love? I tasted the word, tested it in the corners of my brain, fought to let the word collide with an image of Josh. He couldn't *like* me anymore, much less feel something bigger than that. I've spent years making sure of it. I made a soft sound and lowered the bottle.

"I loved Chelsea."

Charlie put his arm around me and tucked me to him. We were still sitting that way when Josh returned, a few minutes before the class got out. I tried to catch his eye, a silent—what? Sorry for being insane? Sorry I can't be the girl you want me to be? —but he wouldn't look at me and I felt strangely timid about talking to him.

The nasty stuff was so much easier to get out.

We went back into Vivian and waited at the end of the hall.

"What now?" I asked Charlie.

"We'll follow him. Try to talk to him."

"When he says 'we,' he means *we*." Josh spat the words at me, pointing to himself and Charlie.

"You're not going without me."

"He's right," Charlie said. "Carter knows what you look like. He'll get nervous if you're following him. And you're not wearing the right shoes." I waited for Josh to give me an I-told-you-so look, but that would require him looking at me again.

"You're not leaving me behind. I found the guy."

Josh spun around. Looked at me. Finally. But that wasn't the way I wanted him to look at me.

"Just once," he hissed. "Just *once* could you not think of yourself first?"

My mouth opened, devoid of words, and he turned away again.

The door opened.

"Which one, Katie?" Charlie asked.

I watched, cheeks burning with indignation. "That one. Blue t-shirt."

Josh and Charlie took off, walking together at a pace that hinted they've been doing this sort of thing forever. Like spy-games-stalking was part of boys' DNA or something. Down the stairs after Carter. Out of sight.

I hurried to the first floor and watched them cross the plaza. They disappeared around a corner and down another flight of stairs. No. I wouldn't stay. I pulled my shoes off and rushed behind, the concrete of the steps digging into the balls of my feet as I descended. I saw Charlie's hands ball into a fist before he leaped at Carter and pinned him to a wall. Josh pulled Charlie off and the three of them disappeared behind a dumpster on a loading dock.

I had to see this. I had to know. I had to take him down myself. He could be the one. He was the one, I knew it. Killer. Murderer. We found him.

I ran to the shadowy dock, not caring who told me to stay behind, not caring why he would tell me to stay behind. When

I rounded the corner of the dumpster, I froze. They were right there. Charlie, his arm bulging and his face red, held Carter to the wall. They pelted him with questions.

Where were you last Sunday night?

How did you know Chelsea?

Were you stalking her?

Why did you kill her?

Carter looked from Charlie to Josh, his eyes wide and desperate. He sputtered answers to their questions. "I don't know a Ch . . . I was studying . . . Kill? What are you . . . ? Who are you? Help!" He reached into his pocket with shaking hands and pulled something out.

"Careful!" Josh shouted, swiping at Carter's hand. There was a clang and a tube rolled to me, stopping at my feet. I picked it up and read the label.

My shoulders sagged. My soul sagged. Why couldn't it have been him? I almost didn't say anything, just to watch them terrorize Bryant, to see someone beat to a pulp for Chelsea, even if he didn't kill her. Someone needed to pay and nobody was and it made me sick. But so would letting this thing with Charlie and Josh and Carter happen.

"He didn't do it," I whispered to the garbage blowing past my ankle. Then louder, "Put him down. It wasn't him."

Charlie and Josh looked at me, but neither backed off Carter. Carter's wheezing accelerated and his face drained of all color. "Charlie!" I yelled. Carter fell to the ground and I went to him. Handed him his inhaler.

We watched him suck at the medicine and take several slow, deep breaths.

"This is assault," he gasped. "I have a lawyer."

"Did you know Chelsea Mathis?" I asked him, watching him struggle to his feet. I wasn't ready to help him up, yet. I wasn't completely ready to believe it wasn't him. He glared at me.

"I don't know who you're talking about. I'm calling the cops." He pulled again at his inhaler and fumbled for his phone. Josh snatched it out of his hand just as he entered his passcode. "We'll mail it back to you."

Carter yelled at us as we walked away, but he didn't seem to be stable enough to follow us.

"There's no way he could have overtaken Chelsea. She would have kicked his ass," Charlie said. "I guess I knew that when I realized he probably weighed less than Chelsea did. But I feel like I have to blame someone." He clutched strands of hair between his fingers. "*Everyone*."

"I know. Me, too."

He walked us back to my car, where I hugged him tightly, hanging on until the wave of disappointment, the wave of fear, faded from me.

"I'll keep trying," I whispered.

"Maybe . . . maybe we should let it go. Trust that the cops know what they're doing. Go home and get some sleep, Katie. Call me soon, though. Love you."

Josh was already going through Carter's phone when I got into the car and pulled out of the garage.

"Anything?"

He shook his head.

"Josh . . . "

He shook his head again.

"I'm sorry."

"Save it for when you mean it."

I peeked at him as I drove. He continued to search the phone for anything useful. I faced forward, biting the inside of my mouth. Focused on oxygen.

I wished, for a moment, I could let him in.

I wished I could let myself go.

14

I didn't love this Tuesday the way I normally love Tuesdays. I banged Carolina's bedroom door shut the next morning and tried to ignore the ribbons that littered the hallway on this, the one week anniversary of Chelsea's infamous coming out of the closet. Stacey wore two ribbons, one on each shoulder, and had several tied around her purse. I was surprised she didn't have them decorating her hair or taking the place of her shoelaces. White in one shoe, to symbolize violence against women, and black in the other to symbolize mourning.

I didn't even like being behind a car in traffic that was decked out in those magnet ribbons.

"I have a ribbon for you," Stacey said after I was done eating breakfast. She held the horrid thing out to me like she was offering a puppy a treat, all raised eyebrows and eager smile. I took it gently.

"Thank you," I said. She beamed.

"We made them up last night. We were supposed to be deciding if we wanted to go with bunting on the chairs at the fashion show or if we wanted to leave the bamboo open, but this was just way too important."

"That's so magnanimous of you, to totally put the chair decisions aside in order to commemorate Chelsea's memory."

She flattened under my sarcasm.

"I'm sorry. I'm just . . . " I shook my head. "I hope you were able to figure out the chair thing," We walked down the street.

She waved her hand, brushing aside the "chair thing."

"It doesn't matter in the long run. These are the things that matter. Remembering friends." We split up to go to our separate classes. Once Stacey turned away I balled the ribbon up in my fist.

"Oh, Katie." She twisted around to address me. "What do you think: bunting or no?"

"No," I said automatically. I wanted that to be my automatic response to everything Stacey said anymore. No, no, no. No to your gossip, no to your ribbons. I took a breath. I'd lost Chelsea. Damon and I hung on by a thread. Now Stacey. I was losing friends fast. "The chairs are so pretty unadorned."

"That's what I thought, too. See ya."

She waved as she trotted away. I watched her hand out three more ribbons to eager students before she turned the corner. I counted to ten and searched for my center and entered the lab.

I didn't know how the other students managed it every day, coming here, holding steady, contributing. The effort was excruciating. This work was so detailed, I had to be so focused. But my head was swimming.

I wished I could go back home again, climb into bed, listen to Dad's chef, Guy, playing old Patricia Kaas albums downstairs as he chopped celery and minced garlic.

But I had an image to uphold. My phone buzzed. I snuck a glance at the new professor taking over for Griffin. I'd already forgotten his name. He was reading an article in a magazine while we worked.

Are we done with this time apart thing? Want to go off campus for lunch? My treat.

Damon.

How do you tell someone you don't trust them anymore? That you're scared of things you shouldn't be afraid of?

I think we're done.

Thank God, because I'm missing you. Love you.

A fat, round tear plopped out of my eye and rolled down my cheek. This was Damon. Harmless Damon.

No. I mean, I think we're done.

I didn't know if he would get it. I hoped he did. No, I hoped he didn't. I was the biggest coward of all time. I paused with my thumb over the send button for a long time, staring at the message, staring at my work. I stared, long after the professor began talking again. Stared, even when I knew people were looking at me and wondering why I was so weirdly still. Then I bit the bullet and pressed send.

I closed my eyes. It was silent, silent. The silence crashed in on me. So I focused on my work. When class ended, it wasn't silent. Damon waited for me.

"Holy fuck," he muttered. Then louder. "Fucking shit, Katie."

I felt small and honorless and cowardly. I had just broken up with my boyfriend of the last year and a half over text message. I started walking away and he stumbled after me.

He grabbed my elbow and looked up at me with tortured eyes as I rounded the corner and looked away again just as quickly.

"Shit, Katie," he said, his phone open to the texts in his hand. "What is this?"

"I'm sorry," I choked out.

"You're sorry," Damon repeated dully. He sighed and shuffled away from me, then back to me and I could smell his soap and muscle scent and I could remember how he held me and how goofy he could be and how beautiful we looked together. I felt his kiss, a ghost kiss, and how much he had always wanted me.

"Am I supposed to get it? Why this is happening? Was it something I did? Or didn't do? Because I can work on it, whatever it is."

I wished he would simply be angry. Angry and mean and screaming at me and cussing at me so that it didn't have to hurt like this, so that I didn't have to feel like I was tearing out his heart and serving it back to him on a plate. Angry and yelling so that I could stop him from looking at me with that vulnerable look and instead flip him off and tell him to go screw himself and that I was better off without him. Scream at him to just *tell me* he didn't do it, as if that would make everything better.

But it would not be so easy.

"It's not you," I said.

He gave me a humorless smile.

"That's what you say, right, when it really is the other person but you don't want to hurt their feelings? At least you still care about my feelings."

I stepped even closer to him and put my arms around him and it felt safe and normal, so much so that I almost asked if I could take it all back.

"I care about your feelings," I said. "I care about you. I really do. This just isn't what I need right now. I need time. And space."

"I thought I was giving you space."

"It wasn't enough."

He absorbed that information and reluctantly pulled my arms away from him and stepped back.

"Can't we just . . . I can do a better job giving you space."

"I don't think that would be a good idea," I whispered. "Chelsea . . ."

"This is about Chelsea? Really? God, Katie. It's always about Chelsea. It used to feel like a battle to get your attention from her, sometimes. She's not even alive anymore and I'm still battling."

I flinched like he'd slapped me.

"How can you say that?" I could hardly get the words out, my chest ached so much.

"Doesn't matter, does it? Anything I say."

Damon gave a jerk of the head that doubled as a nod and walked away. I watched him move down the hallway, watched him slam into people to get them out of his way. The ones, at least, who didn't move aside quickly enough for someone like him. And most of them did.

#

Stacey cornered me in the DG kitchen the next morning.

"Hey, lady," she said.

"Hey, yourself." I took a bite of toast.

Stacey cleared her throat. It wasn't a big I have news kind of clearing. It was hesitant and quiet. Carolina came in and put her own bread in the toaster, watching us out of the corner of her eyes.

"Katie?"

I clenched my hands into fists. Released them.

"Yes, Stacey?" I cooed.

She eyed Carolina uncomfortably.

"I was wondering."

"Yes?"

Stacey opened the fridge and pulled out a soda. She tapped the top of it with her manicured nails.

"SinceDamonandyouareoverdoyouthinkit'sallrightwouldyoumindifIaskedhimtotheSpringCarnivalcelebration?"

Carolina gasped but I suppressed a wild urge to laugh.

"What is wrong with you?" Carolina hissed. "This is not Delta Gamma behavior. Who are you anymore? If we weren't already seniors . . ."

She would have been out, I thought. Because sisters didn't do this kind of thing to each other. And yeah, Stacey had always been a little self-centered, but she usually made up for it in her own way. A little package left near your bedside the morning after a fight or taking everyone out for lunch so she could deliver a dramatic apology. Exes weren't off-limits exactly, but it hadn't even been a full twenty-four hours. Was her boldness because our lives here at UCLA were coming to a close and she was ready to move on? I didn't understand that. Sisters were forever. At least, the way my heart was aching at her words told me so. I tried to bury that emotion, that vulnerability to anything she could say to me.

"What?" Stacey whined. "The party's a week away, and I don't have a date and now Damon doesn't either and so it makes sense for us to go. As friends, of course."

That desire to laugh. Again. Stacey had always, always lusted after my boyfriend. My ex-boyfriend. How irritated with her did I have to be to say *Go for it, hope you're still alive at the end*?

"They just broke up," Carolina continued. "God, you don't do that to your friends."

I looked at Carolina fondly. But Stacey wasn't doing anything really, *really* wrong. Why shouldn't she be allowed to be happy, even though I was miserable? At least she was asking if it was okay, first.

"It's all right with me," I said softly. "Just stay safe, okay?"

"We all have to stay safe," Stacey said. "Always." She hugged me and I felt like giving her my blessing was the first right thing I'd done in a long time.

#

I thought I drove home. That was the only reason I could come up with for why I stood on the sidewalk in front of my house with my car keys in hand and all the lights off. And I didn't mean in the house.

It was an unsettling feeling to be somewhere but be hazy on the how you got there details. My car was parked in the street behind me and I was in one piece still, so that was good.

The sun heated my scalp to an almost burn. It hurt and felt good at the same time.

Josh stared at me. I had no idea when he had shown up, but there he was. He held his car keys, too.

I faced him.

"I'm worried about you," he answered to the question I never asked.

I squinted at him.

"Want to go for a drive?"

I nodded.

I handed him my keys and got into the passenger seat of my own car. I didn't trust myself behind the wheel right now.

Josh got in and adjusted the driver's seat back and drove. We headed west. Then a bit north. Exactly where I wanted to go. He pulled off at Topanga and parked, and we sat in the car for a while watching the waves roll in. He opened the driver's door and came around and opened mine too. I pulled off my shoes and joined him on the blacktop, but flopped back in the seat the moment my toes hit the ground.

"Too hot."

I reached for my shoes, but before I could put them on he pulled me out of the car and slung me over his shoulder.

"Put me down!"

"Be quiet, Katie. Learn to accept a little help."

"This is not help. This is cavemannery. Put me down, you ape!"

He ignored my demands and my fists pounding his back and carried me across the parking lot, bumping my stomach sickeningly against his shoulder, to the sand, to the ocean, and plopped me down at the spot where the saltwater licked the earth.

I glared at him. He tried to hide a smile. I glared harder before looking away.

In the distance, a hazy gray military carrier floated towards San Diego. I searched for a girl with amazing thick hair and dancing eyes.

"Do you remember when Simon died?" I said. Everything felt . . . soft, all of a sudden. The beach breeze took the edge off of everything.

"Yeah," he replied. "I remember."

"All of it?"

"Yeah."

"Why do you keep doing this? Putting up with me when I treat you like crap?"

He inhaled. Paused. By the time he opened his mouth to answer, I didn't want to hear it. I didn't want to hear him say all the things that were wrong with me.

"Never mind."

Josh settled into the sand next to me, studying the keys on my key ring. He looked at the silver "K" for a long time. It had been a present from my mom on my high school graduation. The little blue box came instead of her, even though she'd promised she'd come. An emergency had come up, with a patient. She cured kids with cancer. As many as she could. Not the one she'd needed to years ago, but, sometimes I can imagine how happy other older sisters—faraway sisters—were because of her. And I longed to be them. Who was I to complain that Mommy couldn't be at my graduation when she was out saving lives? It was just another day, anyway. I couldn't be so selfish to let her absence bother me.

"What are you thinking about?"

My mom.

Death.

How selfish I was.

"It's none of your business."

It was the wrong thing to say.

"Look, if you don't want me here, don't want me around, stop bringing up stuff that we used to . . . just stop asking for favors. I'm not your maid."

"It's not like that. I do . . . I mean, I want you around. I just can't . . . don't you get it? Everything that happened, you were there. How do I get over it if you're always around?"

"You get over it by dealing. You grieve. You don't push away the people who care."

"You care?" He gave me an impatient look. I dropped my voice, a strange shyness coming over me. "I care, too. You have to believe me."

"You don't make it easy to."

"It's complicated. I have to be . . ." *Perfect*, I was going to say. Perfect so that people didn't underestimate me. Perfect so that my dad didn't worry about me. Perfect so that I could be a good example to my sorority sisters. Perfect so that . . . my Mom could be proud. Come back. See me for the first time in four years. Remember that, once upon a time, she'd had *two* children.

But I wasn't a child anymore.

He took my hand, suddenly and with a sharpness that wasn't mean, but was something else. My body trembled under his touch. A swift reaction that took my breath away.

"You *make* it complicated."

He tugged me to him and, this. This was what I'd wanted all along. I could feel his breath on my cheeks. Our limbs matched up. He was tall, but I was, too. Perfectly matched. The heat of him sunk into my skin. I wanted to release, let myself fall into his arms, into his sweet heart. To stare into those penetrating eyes for hours, until he'd unraveled all the secrets of my soul. I craved his touch on my back, my hips, my face.

His eyes were so close, locked onto mine. I couldn't look away. He licked his lips. His thighs burned against mine. I tipped my chin up, but stopped with just a beach breeze between us.

I wanted Josh like I'd never wanted Damon. Like I'd never wanted anyone else. But want was this thing I'd learned to control. Something—someone—can't leave you if you didn't want it in the first place.

I sensed his confusion at the way I hesitated. The way he began to speak, but didn't. Collected, rearranged his thoughts, then tried again.

"You're a lot like your mom. You blame yourself if you can't save everyone. I don't want you doing that to yourself all the time."

I yanked my hand away and turned my back to him so I didn't have to see him looking at me as though he could fix me. As though there was anything wrong in the first place. As though he wasn't part of the problem.

"You don't know what you're talking about," I snapped.

And that was the last of that. The last time I would bring it up. What was I doing here? With him? Had I really just broken up with my boyfriend, really just shattered the perfect relationship I'd built? Why was I rushing headlong into this great ruination of everyone's lives?

It had to stop. I spun back around.

"Take me home."

"Katie, don't."

He had a right to be frustrated. I was a nut. We couldn't be easy to deal with.

"Take me home. Get in the car and drive me home. And when we get there, go back to Triangle and leave me alone. For good."

He twisted my keys around his finger a couple of times.

"I'm not going to put up with this forever, Katie."

"Okay." I bit my lip. "You remember everything? Growing up next door to me. Going to school together. Getting our UCLA acceptances." I trailed off, glossing over all the other things we'd done together. All the things he'd once been to me. "I feel like we've done so much together. Remember when Simon got sick? When you said everything would be okay? It wasn't. You lied to me."

He flinched liked I'd struck him. My chest screamed in silent pain when he turned those agonized eyes on me. How could I keep blaming him for something he didn't do? I couldn't keep treating him this way. And he couldn't keep reminding me of everything I wanted, but couldn't have, didn't get. That's why I wanted him out of my life. For good.

15

The ball machine was already on the court when I got back to my house. Dad must have been practicing. I was glad he was keeping in good shape.

I went out in my tennis clothes, racket held firmly in hand, and programmed the machine for fast. Random angles. Variable spins. I had studying to do, but instead I took my place on the opposite side of the court and waited. Waited for that first blast of pink and green color to burst out of the machine.

I swung at the first ball and sent it over the fence. I did the same with the second, and the third. I let the fourth ball go by me as I adjusted my grip on my racket, focused my attention. The next fifty serves I returned with precision, studied grace and talent. Each time my racket connected with the ball I felt it in my arms, my chest, my lungs.

I raced across the court side to side, drenching my clothes with sweat as the sun beat down upon me. I hit another fifty, then another fifty. My hands and elbows ached but I didn't stop until all three hundred balls were gone from the machine.

I sat on the hot court and looked at the mass of tennis balls against the far fence and conjured my best friend beside me, because I wanted nothing else right then.

"Your form is excellent," she'd said last month.

"It should be, after all those years of lessons."

Chelsea had wrangled my racket from my grasp.

"I hate tennis."

"I know. You'll never play with me," I'd pouted.

"You intimidate me."

"Whatever."

She'd flung my tennis racket toward the net like it was a throwing knife. We'd watched it flip, head over handle, before settling on its side in front of the net with a shudder.

"How's it going with Damon?"

I'd pulled my knees up and buried my face in them. "Fine. Same as usual."

"Is the usual fine?"

I'd shrugged. The sun had reflected off the court, got caught in the area under her eyes. Glowed.

"I guess so."

"You don't really open up to him," Chelsea had insisted. She'd gotten up and retrieved the racket. Handed it to me. "You're stronger than you think. When things come at you, at speeds the rest of us shy away from, you swing at them. Like you're this great force and nothing could penetrate you. Maybe that's a problem."

"Thanks for the Zen thought of the day, Buddha. While you're in the mood for dispensing priceless tidbits of wisdom, you want to tell me why you've been so sick lately?"

Chelsea swept her hair back and peeked at me through half-lidded eyes. "Food poisoning."

"Gross. Just don't puke on me. I don't want your icky germs everywhere." I'd pushed my shoulder into her leg so that she toppled over onto the ground.

Now, I wonder how I could have missed all the signs. How I could have let her get away with a silly answer like food poisoning. I was going to be a scientist. I should have known better.

The patio doors opened. Across the yard my father waved at me from his vantage point on the deck. I waved back and stood up, retrieving my racket, and headed over to him.

"Hello, dear," he said, giving me a fond kiss on the head. "I didn't expect to see you midweek. A nice surprise. This was left on our porch. Know anything about it?"

He held out an envelope and three tennis balls. I took the items.

"Yeah. Thanks." I launched the tennis balls toward the court and stuffed the envelope in my pocket. "Hey, Dad? Let's go out tonight. Do you have plans? We can get some sushi. Or some of that horrible Caribbean food you love."

He gave the backyard a fleeting, worried glance and nodded at me.

"That sounds good. Okay, Katie. I'll make a call and cancel an appointment and we can go out. As long as you can handle being out in public with a man as old as I am."

"You're not so bad. Any girl would be proud of you."

I dressed up. Decked myself out in a strappy, red, Latin inspired mini-dress (Dad picked the awful Caribbean place, but at least it had dancing), strapped on four inch heels and pinned a flower bigger than my ear to the side of my hair. I puckered up at myself in the mirror. Yes, this was what I needed. Powerful red, powerful Katie.

The night was intoxicating. Dad strutted me into the restaurant on his arm as the sun set as though it was a red carpet we walked down. I ate rice and sweet potatoes, and the bartender I made eyes at all night sent over a strawberry margarita and mojito. After dessert, Dad excused himself to take an emergency business call because his appointment just refused to be cancelled, but I told him I would stay and get a taxi home later. After he kissed my cheek and left, I went over to the bar and downed two shots of tequila straight. I then leaned over the bar and kissed the bartender on the mouth and danced with the first, second and third boy that asked. I shook my ruffles to the music.

Chelsea would have loved it, this night. She would have loved dancing with me and she would have made it a game to see who could kiss the most boys. She would have worn a red flower in her hair, just like mine. I looked up into the lights on the ceiling and imagined she was the one with her hands on my waist.

Boy number three was dragging me out the door when the bartender caught me at the door.

"There you are," he said, like he knew me. He glared at boy number three, who backed off quickly and disappeared into the crowd on the dance floor.

I pouted. "You have to dance with me now because you scared the boy away."

He took my hands and I stepped to the music and almost fell over but he put his arm around me and kept me from falling. "I take pride in making sure drunk girls don't go home with creepy guys. I already called you a cab."

"You're very sweet. I mean that, I really do." I blew kisses to my boys, to the bartender, to the booth of ladies at the front of the restaurant who shot me dark looks because I was so much hotter than they could ever hope to be. I stumbled a little.

I could hear Dad yelling at someone through his office door, so I didn't disturb him. Guy helped me to my room.

"Thank you, Guy," I slurred. I sat on my bed and took off my shoes. Guy kissed my hand and turned off the light with a last, stern look and said good night. I stern-looked him back, but I wasn't ready for bed. I needed a drink of water.

I went through my closet to my bathroom and filled a glass. Then I stumbled back, kicking the tennis clothes I'd worn earlier and had left on the floor. The skirt flew across the room. I grasped at a closet rod to keep from splashing my water everywhere.

An envelope fell out of the skirt pocket.

I picked it up and settled myself on the floor and crossed my legs while my dress hiked up to my hips. Carefully, as though it was the most precious thing on earth, I focused my reeling brain on the envelope and slit it open. The note inside was short.

I thought you should know. Another dog has fallen sick. Wookie, the Yorkshire. Olga wants us to come down to the shelter tomorrow to pick out a new dog for the show. Let me know if you'd rather drive yourself. Josh.

"Aw, not Wookie," I whispered, trying and failing to remember what the dog looked like from the stack of photos. I realized that second shot of tequila might not have been a good idea. And maybe not the first one, either.

It took a few minutes, and a lot of help from my drawer handles, but I got to my feet. I stumbled out of my room and leaned heavily on the banister as I descended the stairs.

"I'm going next door, Dad," I said into the general direction of the downstairs. I assumed he heard me even though he didn't answer.

The night was still warm, but it was dark and crickets warbled in the grasses and hedges and flowers. I hadn't a clue what time it was. When I reached Josh's front porch there were no lights on inside. I didn't want to wake them, so I took the pebble path around the side of the house—the ant path—and retrieved the key that had been under the same yard art since the house was built, probably, back in the dark ages. I unlocked the gate and slipped into the backyard, gathering tiny pebbles in my fist from the planters and pots that were scattered along the walkway as they caught my eye.

I tripped over a patch of grass and went down on all fours. I thought about staying there, curling up into the softness of the lawn and sleeping under the stars. It was lovely here, with the bug chirps in my ears and the moon winking at me. But no, I was on a mission. Never even thinking he wouldn't be at home. Would have returned to campus.

I rose to my feet purposefully and walked. Once positioned under Josh's window I took a pebble, raised my arm, and flung the missile upward. It missed by several feet, thunking against the side of the house and torpedoing back down to nail me in the shoulder.

"Ouch," I complained loudly.

I tried again and got closer the second time, despite the stumble. The next toss was spot on, pinging against the glass. I threw another one, unsure whether he had heard that last one or not. Another bulls-eye. His light went on. He appeared on his balcony. I giggled and flung my arms out to him.

"Romeo, Romeo." I lost my balance as I looked up at him and tripped over my own feet, falling sloppily to the grass. "Let down your hair," I finished with a flourish from the ground.

He disappeared back into his room and I pouted. But the next moment he was there, right next to me, in his boxers and his sleep mussed hair.

"You're still here. Your hair is just. So. Cute." I lurched forward to muss it up further, but he caught my wrist and held me away from him.

"You smell like a liquor cabinet," he said.

"A liquor cabinet? What a funny phrase!" I leaned in, despite his hand holding me back. It was such a delicious feeling. Such a freeing feeling to not be able to hold back my thoughts. They would come out whether I wanted them to or not. "You're always so, so funny," I sneered.

He dropped my wrist and took a few steps back.

"No, wait," I cried out, knowing I was here for a reason, struggling to find it. "Wookie! I got your note about Wookie. Poor girl. Is she all right?"

He considered me for a moment. I couldn't take my eyes off his bare shoulders. I reached my fingers to them, grasping only air. They seemed so much closer.

"I haven't heard since earlier," he said, giving in to my question. "But you should go home. Go to bed."

"Why are you here? Why aren't you at Triangle?"

He shrugged, like he didn't want to tell me.

"You're keeping an eye on me, aren't you? That's. So. Sweet." I paused. "I think I'm going to throw up."

He took another step back, but I froze. There was this something, this question, and these *things*, rolling around in the back of my head. Something about puke and spit and a shirt, but I couldn't put the pieces together because as soon as I grasped at one, the rest swam away. I sucked in a breath of cold air and shook the sickness out of my head. "No, s'okay. I feel better now."

I took a step toward him. And another, until I was in his space again.

"I broke up with Damon," I slurred.

"Okay. Katie, you need a shower. And some sleep."

"No, I've had a wonderful night and I don't want it to end. The guy with the sprayer thing was so sweet. First he gave me a strawberry thing and then a lime thing and then Dad said no more. But then Dad went away and he didn't know about the other two things. I can't remember what they were called. Do you remember? No? And then, I kissed the guy with the sprayer and danced with aaaaalll the boys. They wanted to take me home, all of them," I boasted.

"I bet they did," Josh admitted, holding my arms so I wouldn't topple us both over.

"Do you know what?" I asked, moving in closer to him, sinking into his expression. I batted my smoky eyes at him. Felt the way his fingers seared my skin with heat. The way my legs were weak, but with wanting him, not with alcohol. Had I always wanted him this much? Was I holding back before? Of course I was. Protecting my heart when I knew he could steal it if I let down my guard.

But now wasn't about my heart. Now was about my body, my stomach pressed against his firm abs, our thighs pressed together, his gorgeous eyes watching me closely. My breath came quickly and I said what I'd wanted to say for a long time, but was afraid to say: "I want to kiss you, too. I wanted to kiss you at the beach. Remember that? Can I kiss you, Josh?"

His grasp on my arms firmed.

"No."

"Yes."

I closed my eyes and waited for his kiss. It never came. He bypassed my lips and went straight for my ear.

"You're the most beautiful drunk I've ever seen," he whispered to me in a short burst of air, the motion of it tickling my ear. He pushed me away from him. "But we're not friends, remember? Go home, Katie, and sleep it off."

And he left me there. He walked away and left me there alone on his lawn.

16

Classes were out of the question for the next day. I slept in, in my own bed, since there was no way I could drive back to the sorority, squinted against the mid-day sun and fought against a headache that threatened to rip my skull apart when I finally woke. Guy made me a mug of black coffee (ew) and set it on the kitchen counter with two aspirin.

"Thanks, Guy," I said to him once I'd showered and come downstairs. Mina, the housekeeper, hovered in the background, not wanting to turn the vacuum on. "Was I so awful?"

"No, not too awful," Guy assured me. "You were stunning. You reminded me of a night I spent in tiny Bega de Mar, in Espania, before I came to cook for you. I was cooking for another family that vacationed there and on the last night of the vacation all the boys and girls from the town and the farms and the hotels came together to dance and eat and sing and drink. The girls all wore flowers and ruffles, like you did last night. They were a vision. I fell in love with each of them, all at the same time, and the sea made us all drunk."

Guy pulled a bowl out of a cupboard and changed the tone of his voice. "I'm not sure that any of them became as sloppy as you, though," he lectured. "There is a difference between a little something that makes one's eyes sparkle and something more that makes everyone worried that you are going to throw up on them."

I closed my eyes and let his words sink in.

"I know," I mumbled.

I pressed my fingers to my forehead and swore off drinking forever. I didn't relate to Guy the rest of what happened that night, but not even the alcohol could keep it from my memory. I knew, and I couldn't take it back, that I went to Josh's. And it was a disaster. If everything else from last night was a blur, I remembered that part in crystal clarity. I wished I couldn't.

I felt closer to human after a short afternoon nap and the four tall glasses of water Guy forced upon me. Realizing I had lost my own personal PI, I went into the office and sat in front of the computer screen with no clue how to begin finding information about Sigma2992.

I typed it into Google and hit enter, but the scarce results, half of them in languages other than English (and the rest in tech-speak or something, so pretty much the same thing), didn't look too promising. I dropped my face into my hands and thought about going back to sleep. I was useless.

"I'm sorry, Charlie," I mumbled into my fingers.

When the doorbell rang I was in the middle of trying out different combinations of the username (one page of search results were far better, I'd decided, than the bazillion Sigma alone pulled). Mina answered the door and I listened as she led Josh into the office. I probably looked like a goblin, hunched over the computer keyboard, fending off the remnants of my hangover. But he didn't say anything to me. He just stormed at me silently and held up his keys, as if that was supposed to mean something.

I closed my eyes.

"The shelter," I whispered.

He retreated outside to wait in his car.

I had to ride with him, because I realized that I didn't know how to get there myself. I supposed I could have asked him to write down the directions or draw me a map, but I loathed the idea of having to search for it with the perma-throb that thumped in my head. So I rode with him.

But had I known he would refuse to turn the music down on the ride there, I would have asked for the map. I shot him the fiercest of glares I could muster, but I would not be the first to speak. We were in the throes of an unspoken no-speaking battle, and I would not surrender.

At the shelter, we walked up and down pet holding area, looking at all the dogs waiting for their new home. My heart broke a million times over.

Olga walked in after a short while.

"Sorry I'm late. How long have you been here?" She addressed Josh.

Josh paused and glanced at his watch.

"About forty minutes," he snapped.

Olga looked slightly taken aback and narrowed her eyes at me suspiciously. Oh, yeah. I wanted to shout at her. It was all *my* fault he was in a pissy mood. Like he was all perfect and never snotty or holier than thou or any of those things.

But I held my tongue.

Olga watched for another minute. "Did you find another dog that would work?"

We both nodded and pointed to the Maltese mix a few cages down.

"Okaaay." She rolled her eyes at us and left us alone in our thick silence.

We spoke as little as possible for the next hour as we took final measurements. When we headed out, I suffered the re-emergence of my hangover headache. Josh kept the radio in his car at just the right volume to enhance my pain double fold. Jerk.

Once back in Beverly Hills, Josh barely slowed down long enough in front of my house to let me get out and slam the door behind me. Then he pulled away again, passing by his own house, determined to reach destinations unknown. I got in my Mini and returned to DG.

#

The subdued feeling that had sat over DG house like a thunder cloud the past week broke up under the excitement of the fashion show dress rehearsals Friday night. The DG ladies packed their outfits and loaded into cars for the drive up to the arena. Even I was excited to see what Triangle had done to transform the space.

The arena looked nothing like it had before.

The catwalk stretched into the center of the arena, but not in a straight line. It curved like a sidewalk. In fact, as I approached it, I realized it was built and painted to look like a sidewalk, too. Fake trees line up against the backdrop and two fire hydrants perched on the catwalk. The Delta Gamma girls ooh'd and ahh'd at everything. As a smile crept over my face, the main lights went out and colored spotlights dotted the stage. Across the back curtain, lights in a Dalmation pattern swam. It was perfect.

"Josh!" Carolina squee'd as he walked out from behind the curtain with several Triangle guys. "It's awesome!"

"Amazing," I said.

He just looked at me once, silently, and then back at Carolina.

"Thanks, Carolina." Not a single word from him for me. Fine.

I spun around, my back to him. "Ladies! Let's get changed."

We gathered in the temporary changing room to put on our outfits. I tried to forget that Josh was mere feet away as I stripped down. My designer chose a sweeping silk gown for me in black that would be beautifully offset by the white American Eskimo mixed breed I was now partnered with during the fashion show. The little pup was wearing a silk bow tie and teeny top hat that hooked under his chin with elastic. When I saw the ensemble, I gathered the dog in my arms, not caring about hair in my dress and cuddled him. Too adorable.

One by one, the DG girls held leashed dogs as they sashayed down the catwalk to a recording of Courtney's band's music. The brilliance of the lights made it hard to see the sea of chairs beyond the catwalk, but Josh stood close enough that I saw the way his eyes swept over my body as I moved past him. And the way they looked away quickly.

I also saw the way Tommy Yan grinned at Carolina. And her shy smile back at him as I headed off the catwalk.

We undressed and carefully packed our clothing again. The girls were beaming. I was, too. Partly for me, but for Chelsea, too. This had been her idea and it was going off flawlessly. We'd sold out the event and the excitement was palpable. It must have been the exhilarating feeling still pumping through my veins that prompted me to speak to Josh before we headed back to campus. Nothing else could have done it. I did not put things out there, out in the open, like Chelsea used to.

"Are you going to drop this whole silent treatment thing any time soon? It's so childish."

He answered by scowling as he wrapped a cord around his forearm.

"Pouting is so unattractive," I continued, pulling my hair out of my face. His glance fell on someone over my shoulder.

Olga walked toward us. "How'd it go?"

"Super!" I said. Olga stumbled over a cord. Her bag went flying out of her hands, half of its contents spilling on the ground around us. Josh and I automatically bent to pick it all up. Our faces were suddenly so close. I flushed with heat. I'd swear I'd never been in such a tight place before.

My heart pounded as I pulled back and wrapped my hand around Olga's keys. The ring was huge, almost industrial-sized, with an army of metal-toothed soldiers. Between Olga being able to get into anywhere and Stacey knowing everyone, they could rule the world.

Before I stood up again, I felt Josh take a breath, almost as though he was going to say something. I froze, waiting for his words. But all he did was let the air out again. I passed Olga's things to her, grabbed my bag, and nearly ran to the parking lot.

If that was the way he wanted it between us, I could deal.

Doing all this without Chelsea? That's what was tearing my heart apart. She was supposed to be on that catwalk with me. Flaunting. Teasing. Having an awesome time. There weren't any more big events after this. A few more parties. Finals. Graduation. Then, that was it. It was all over. Four years of it.

And suddenly I felt that I couldn't do it. Couldn't go out into the world without my best friend beside me. I couldn't. My energy fled, and my knee ached where I had injured it ages and ages ago playing tennis.

I slowed at a stoplight.

I knew what she would say.

"Of course you can do it, K. Why else would you have worked so hard for those perfect grades? For this, right? To head off to Stanford and show them all what a gorgeous big, fat brain you have."

But she was supposed to be here, too. My sister, my best friend. When the light turned green, I kept driving, dreading the future I was heading into, alone.

#

Some of the Triangle fraternity guys met back at our place for a good luck pre-fashion show party. In the corner of the backyard where the keg was set up, Stacey steadily pounded plastic cups full of beer while random boys watched. I grimaced. I hated that there was tension in the DG house now. I hated that I didn't know how to fix it, or even if I would have time to before graduation. I wanted to go off into the world knowing the DG ladies were supporting me, and them knowing they could still call on me for whatever they needed.

An hour into the fiasco I found Carolina sitting on the front porch, shaking her head at someone peeing in the flower beds.

"Ew," I said as I sat down next to her. "Do you think that'll kill the flowers?"

"I don't know. I would hope so, if I were those flowers."

Pee guy zipped his jeans and returned to the house, passing us with a suave, "Hello ladies." We saluted him as one.

"Chelsea would have gone over and kicked him in the ass while his pants were still down," I said.

"Yup. She would have."

"I missed her today. Felt wrong to be on the catwalk without her."

"I know. I missed her too, K." Carolina rested her head on my shoulder. "Do you think the janitor really did it?"

I thought back to my conversation with Charlie and how neither one of us knew what to think about the arrest. Maybe because it didn't answer any of our questions. It just created more. But it had gotten me wondering why that DNA was found on the janitor.

"I don't know. It seems, weird, you know? I mean, they found her DNA on his clothes and everything, but Chels was sick in that bathroom a lot. What if it was just her puke on his shirt?" I closed my eyes against the nagging feeling that came every time I considered these things. "I don't know what to think. Really, he was just this quiet guy who cleaned up after us slobs."

"Yeah. But sometimes it's the quiet ones you have to watch, right? I guess that's what the police are for. Figuring all that stuff out so we don't have to."

"I suppose." I gave her a squeeze and stood up. "Things have been . . . awful, lately. I'm sorry I haven't been the same Katie. Sorry things aren't great."

"We understand, Katie. Considering what happened, I think you've been incredible."

I smiled at her, my muscles relaxing a bit. "Thanks, Lina. I'm going to head upstairs. All these boys, you know?"

"I'm surprised Josh didn't come by."

I tugged on a piece of hair and shrugged. I wasn't. "Who needs Josh when you have . . ." I glanced around. "Tommy Yan?"

Carolina blushed in the dim light of the porch.

"Tommy's taking me to the Carnival celebration."

Inside the house someone had increased the volume on the stereo and bad '80s house music thumped against the wall.

"Nerdy Triangle engineer Tommy?"

Carolina let her arms dangle over her knees.

"Yeah, nerdy Triangle engineer Tommy." She looked at her bracelet, dangling on her wrist and gave a self-deprecating laugh. "He's really nerdy."

"So?" I squinted at her. I know what it's like to be judged for one's looks. "We like who we like, right? He's funny . . . in kind of a goofy way, but still. And if he's good for you, then I like him. Who cares what people think?"

Carolina nodded. "I do like him, K. He makes me laugh, and I need that right now. And he's cute . . . in that goofy way."

"He has very nice legs," I agreed. I should know good legs, since I couldn't stop thinking about Josh's. "Thanks to all the soccer those guys play." I bent down and kissed her cheek.

Carolina swatted at me playfully and I headed upstairs. I got halfway up before I changed my mind, got in my car and drove, ending up at Topanga. I didn't get out of the car. I just sat there for a while and thought about the people I would miss when this year was all over. The brilliant ladies at DG. Professors who had brought me so far. My dad. A boy with haunting, blue-green eyes.

And I thought about the person who hadn't made it to the end of the year. The ache of missing Chelsea tore me apart. I didn't know how I would get through graduation, moving, the next years of my life without her.

The dark settled in around me and permeated my senses with smell and sound, like those shells you hold to your ear and close your eyes and hear nothing but the ocean. I put on music, softly, and drifted to sleep for a while even though I should have been afraid to sleep in a public place like this, in the middle of the night.

But I wasn't afraid.

Chelsea was there with me. Not in body, but in my mind, in my heart, in my memory. Forever. And no one could take that away from me.

At just after two I woke, started the engine again and headed back to campus, hoping the girls hadn't realized I was gone. We did our best to look out for each other. I noticed my phone battery had run down while I slept. But that was all right. The person I wanted to be able to get a hold of me had been there the whole time.

17

Up with the sun Saturday morning, I braced myself for chaos. The show wasn't until six in the evening, but I wanted everything to be perfect and I knew, with a house full of girls and Triangle frat to wrangle, I would need all day.

"No starving yourselves this morning," I announced once I'd made my way downstairs. The sisters were in a tizzy, running around with curlers hanging halfway out of their hair, dressed in half pajama, half pre-show ensembles, and panicking about lost fake eyelashes. I picked up an earring at my feet, dangled it in the air and watched Ingrid run over with a grateful expression to grab it and fling a quick hug around waist. I grinned. These ladies were the best. "You already look fabulous! Every one of you! And you'll need the energy. Think protein! Think electrolytes!"

Just as I had triple-checked to make sure I had everything I needed to take to the arena, and subverted another hundred, more or less, potential catastrophes, my cell rang. I wrinkled my forehead. Damon.

"Hello?"

"Good luck tonight," he said.

"Thanks."

"I'll be there. Watching."

I stifled a sigh. I wish he wouldn't come, but he'd bought a ticket. And it was nice of him to be supportive.

"I hope you enjoy it," I said.

The guys from Triangle were already at the arena, taping cords to the floor and adjusting chairs and lights, when I arrived. I checked my phone. Eight A.M. Olga would be here soon, though the dogs wouldn't arrive until much later. I hung my dress in the changing room and checked on Josh.

"Good morning," I greeted.

"Good morning," he replied in the same lovely tone of voice.

Oh, good. We were going to pretend to be friends today. I could do that. As long as I didn't look at his muscled arms peeking from under his t-shirt sleeves for too long. Or let his comforting voice say too many things. Or be around his familiar, intoxicating scent too often.

"Would you like a granola bar?" He handed one over to me. "We're going to be busy. You'll need your energy."

I took the bar, careful to not let our fingers touch—I didn't need a loss of resolve this early in the morning—and put it in my bag.

"Thank you. But I ate a large breakfast. I'll save this for later."

I followed Josh as he brought out tables for the entryway. Every dark corner we passed seemed to whisper to me to grab my old neighbor, my old *everything*, and duck in for just a moment. My hands itched to slide over his shoulders, down his back, pull him to me. My body was a traitor and it made me cranky.

"Not there," I snapped as he began to unfold the legs of a card table right next to where the registration table had been set up. "That's for the silent auction. It goes in the main arena."

He glowered at me and took the table back inside. I glowered back as I covered it in the gold tablecloths I'd brought. Josh looked like he was trying not to laugh as he left to take care of a sound issue some of the guys were having in the band stage area. I stuck my tongue out at his back. I wanted that ability. To laugh at everything.

Carolina came up to stand beside me. We watched the set-up progress for a few minutes without speaking.

For a few minutes, I tried not to resent Carolina for not being the person I really wanted standing next to me. For not being Chelsea.

Finally, she said, "Nice view, huh?"

"They've done a really good job with the catwalk."

"That's not what I meant." She looked at me pointedly, then at Josh, then back at me. Only Carolina would notice that I'd been staring at his ass this whole time. Soccer players. They were . . . in good shape. But I pretended I didn't notice.

"Boys. I have to keep tabs on them. Make sure everything is absolutely perfect."

Carolina folded her arms across her chest. "Hm."

"What?"

"K, it will be great. Even if it's not perfect. We've raised a ton of money for the shelter through ticket sales already and there will be more to come when we auction off the clothes. Plus, I bet at least half the dogs featured tonight will find new homes before the weekend's over."

"I hope so."

"So stop being so hard on yourself! When you do that, you miss out on the good things right in front of you. Look at you and Josh. You grew up together. You both came to UCLA—totally by coincidence. Both ended up in the Greek system, even though I know you've done your best over the years to avoid him for whatever reason. You've been teamed up on this project. You're both going north after this, for crying out loud."

"What are you talking about?"

"Tommy told me Josh is taking a job offer from a firm in San Francisco. And you'll be at Stanford. So . . . I don't know. Maybe it's a good idea to step back from this idea of perfection, which doesn't exist anyway, and just let fate take over for a while. Let happiness come easy."

Fate. It wasn't the sort of thing a science-loving girl like me believed in. At least, not if I didn't want to get laughed out of my labs. But Carolina's argument was hard to deny. I wasn't sure what to say, so instead I folded her into a surprise hug.

"Thanks for everything, Lina."

"I'm here. A friend. Not the one you want most, I know . . . but a shoulder. If you ever need one."

"Thank you," I repeated softly.

#

That afternoon, Josh and I stood outside, waiting for the second truck to arrive with the other half of the dogs. The first had already been unloaded into the arena and were being groomed and played with by the DG ladies. Smiles abounded. Except between us.

Josh's shoulder was close enough to make me nervous. Everything about the way he stood there, breathed, watched the road, swallowed, made me nervous. Made me want to be even closer. God, his lips were so perfect. I cleared my throat, hoping that would clear my head. But a fire raged in my belly when he was near me. And I didn't have Damon as an excuse anymore.

I closed my eyes and breathed.

"I think I know who killed Chelsea," I stammered, swallowing hard. I had to get this out of me, tell someone who might actually listen. Josh used to always listen. But now he remained stoic, arms crossed against his chest. His eyes were forward, but his pupils didn't follow the action on the road anymore. I knew he'd heard me. "He didn't deny anything when I brought it up to him."

Josh whipped his head toward me. "You accused someone? You stood there and talked to someone you think killed Chelsea. *Again*. Are you crazy?"

"I didn't realize he was the killer at the time," I cried, cutting off as Olga rushed to us with a wild look in her eyes.

"I just got a call from the second driver. He was supposed to swing by my house to pick up special food for one of the dogs but he said the other driver grabbed it. Did you get a paper bag of food out of the first truck?" She looked at me as though I was hiding the food under my shirt.

"No, I didn't see anything like that," I said.

"Katie never sees anything," Josh added.

"What's that supposed to mean?"

"You and Damon get back together again?"

"Heck, no. If you'd listen to me you'd know why. But even if we had, what's it to you?"

"The food!" Olga reminded us, snapping her fingers to get our attention.

"Sorry, Olga," Josh said. "I haven't seen it."

"Josh never sees anything," I finished for him.

"You used to live next door to me. I've seen more than I've ever wanted to."

"What's that supposed to mean?" I repeated.

Olga growled.

"Look," she snapped. "Both of you. Your bickering is getting on my nerves. If that's all you're doing right now, you have time to grab the food. Maybe even time to get a room." She breezed right past my incoherent protests. Josh only snorted. "I'll wait for the truck. Go down Altamont, take a left at 3rd, a right at Cherry, a left on Belmont. Yellow house easy to find. Here," she said, scribbling something on a post-it note and shoving it into Josh's hand. He folded the paper in half without looking at it and stuck it in his pocket. "The address if you get lost. My husband's home and the food should be right on the kitchen counter. If it's not there, he can help you find it."

I started to protest—I couldn't just leave everyone unattended—but she waved us off with the back of her hand and went back inside.

I glared at Josh, ready to resume our argument, but he was already headed toward his car.

"Let's go," he hollered at me, tone dripping with sarcasm. "You can talk about how you know who did it but decided to tell me instead of the police on the way."

We loaded into his car. I folded my arms and glared straight ahead as he cranked up the volume on the stereo. We sped down the road, racing the bullet fast drum beat of the song blaring out of Josh's speakers. It was a perfect soundtrack for my loathing of the boy who sat next to me. And my hatred of the way he made me feel: angry, frustrated, wanting. He took the corners as though we were on a racetrack, skidding around them with a loud screeching sound that frightened pedestrians and sent them cringing away from the road.

"Are you trying to kill us?" I spat, turning my fiercest look-of-hate on him.

"Would you care if I was?" he yelled right back at me.

I made a *hugnh* sound at the back of my throat.

"Well congratulations," I mocked. "You now have the market on melodrama."

He slammed on the brakes as the light ahead of us turned red. I lurched forward in my seat, thrusting my hands out to the dash to stop my forward momentum. I refused to grace his actions with as much as a disgusted look.

"Me?!" he sputtered furiously. "Me? Are you kidding me? There is only one person in this car that worships on the altar of melodrama, and it isn't me."

"Well, it *must* be you because there's only two of us here and it's not *me*." Breathe, Katie, breathe. "What you see is what you get. This is the real deal," I said, my voice calmer, but still thick with derision. We watched the cross street light turned yellow, then red.

"Oh, this is the real Katie, is it?" he said as he pressed on the accelerator again. He didn't finish his thought, but his driving became noticeably saner. He even turned down the volume on the stereo. "This is you?" He paused again and I could almost see the cogs turning in his head. "You're wrong. This isn't real. All the avoidance, all the changing you think you've done." He took a right at a normal speed. "You haven't changed as much as you'd like to think you have. Not in a good way, at least. Just a few stupid things that don't matter much. All you're really doing is hiding."

I rolled my eyes at his psycho babble. Everyone's an armchair shrink.

"Yeah, thanks for that assessment, Dr. Hunter. Real inspired." I watched as we passed a group of kids throwing tricks on a public bike ramp. "How would you know anything about me?"

At the next light Josh took a left, bringing us into a residential neighborhood, and began searching for the yellow house. He pulled to a stop once we reached the cheerful daffodil-colored structure and cut the engine.

He looked at me thoughtfully. His strong jaw and muscular shoulders softening.

"I know, Katie. A lot more than you seem to want me to know. A lot more than you seem to remember that I know." He slouched a little in his seat, propping his elbow on his door and looking out at Olga's house. I watched him reminisce, dreading the memories he was dredging up, dreading the things he could possibly throw at me. "I remember the Katie before her mom took off without a backwards glance and the Katie before that evil stepmother of hers moved in and took over the entire neighborhood—before you thought the right thing to do was be all buddy-buddy with the gold-digging witch, decide to love her and then watch her walk away just like your mom did. And I know the Katie before her little brother died next to her."

He softened all of a sudden, all of him. His voice, his limbs. "I remember Simon, too. Even if you won't talk about him. I remember Katie around Simon. I remember how much you adored him. I miss him, too, you know."

I stared at a house down the road, far in the distance. I tried to memorize the shape, name the insipid blue color. I stared hard. Because I would not cry, I would not. How dare he bring up things that had nothing to do with him? How dare he even utter Simon's name? Just because I brought it up, that one time, did he think it was open season on my memories now?

My insides hurt, burned, like they were filled with hot coals. My voice broke when I started to speak, so I paused, started over again.

"Leave me alone, Josh. Let me be happy the way I know how to be." I shot an angry glance his way because it was easier to be pissed at him than to remember the things I didn't want to think about.

"It could be okay for you to talk about it, you know. Especially since you just lost your best friend."

I looked away from Josh and stared at the blue house again. I counted the houses from here to there. One, two, three, four, five, six, seven. It never took me long to put on a face. I took a breath, let it out.

"Drop it, Josh. You told me things would be okay a long time ago, remember? You were wrong." His body slumped, fatigue in his shoulders. I had to let it go, I knew that, but I couldn't. I needed this anger, this blaming him, to keep from drowning in my other emotions. "Look, let's not argue, okay?"

I flashed him the biggest smile I could manage. He just sat there and stared at me like I was cracked and he didn't respond and he didn't move. I felt the smile fade. And I felt more, more than I wanted to. He forced it out of me, and I was so unwilling to give it up, but there it was and it had always been there, just lurking under the surface, swimming under the façade: my missing mother, the stepmom I had let get too close, Chelsea gone, and a toddler brother who had been the most beautiful thing I had ever seen, the most beautiful soul I had ever known. Who faced his trials with a bravery that made me feel smaller than a flea.

And that promise from that boy I'd cared so much about. That everything was going to okay even though it never was.

Please, I begged my will, *please put it all back. Compartmentalize it again into the dark file I had long hidden it away in. Make it go away. Leave me alone, Josh. Let me be.*

I raised my eyes to his with the intent to tell him off, to scold him again for sticking his nose in places it doesn't belong, but when I caught his eyes, I saw something change in his face, in the expression he was giving me.

And I remembered.

Not just how he said everything would be okay, once upon a time, and then it wasn't. Not just how he watched me at my most vulnerable when my brother died and my mom walked out on me. Not just how he knew all my tender places and all my hurts and all the ways I've been hurt, could be hurt and how much that scared me.

But about how he was always there. How he said, maybe not the right things, but the things he'd hoped would help. How he could, even now, take me down with one well-placed verbal jab, but didn't. Never did. Never would. I wasn't scared of him. I was scared of me. Of letting go and letting him in. Letting anyone in. Josh, Chelsea, my Delta Gamma sisters. Why? He was *Josh*. Despite everything I'd done, all the people I'd tried to keep at bay, he knew me inside out and still cared about me.

My heart grew with understanding until it hurt.

He saw something, too, in my face. Something that changed him, quieted him, finally. And I caught my breath and something else that was rising up in my throat, threatening my composure.

"Josh," I got out.

Except it sounded nothing like it was supposed to sound. It was a whisper. A heart rendering kind of sound. And he heard it, what was there, and what was missing. And he knew what it meant.

He pushed off the door and reached across everything in the middle of us and gathered me up to him, pressing my face into his chest and shh, shh, shhing me again and again as I tried to stiffen my frame, tried to push him away with nothing more than a fading will somewhere in the back of my mind. But the powerlessness overwhelmed me, and the force of the sobs collided with the force of my refusal to cry, to create a shuddering mess of a girl.

It felt so, so good. Letting some of it out. His arms around me. It felt so good that I let it go on longer than I'd meant to. And even then, I wanted more. I wanted time to be with Josh. Time to do-over the years I'd pushed him away. My nose pressed into his neck and he smelled so good. His voice and his touch were so right.

I finally pulled away from him, looking down at the parking brake as I moved back, still hiding. I just couldn't help it. It had become the norm for so long. Avoiding the person who twisted my insides in knots. I unfastened my seatbelt and opened the car door.

"I'll just run in and grab the food, okay?" I said, quietly. "Real quick. I'll be right back."

I fumbled out of the car. Touching the road with my shoe, the firmness of it, was a shock. I drew myself up again.

I knew Josh watched me as I walked onto the sidewalk, passed the mailbox. I knew he watched me as I knocked on the side of the screen door. I knew, knew that he was going to be watching me more closely from now on.

I wasn't sure I minded as much as I used to.

I heard footsteps approach the door from the inside before the knob twisted and the door was pulled back into the shadow of the house. A man stepped forward.

"Katie," Professor Griffin said.

My heart hurt again. But this time, it wasn't the full, delicious ache I'd experienced moments before. This was stabbing pain. A twisting, grinding sensation that made me feel like my chest was caving in.

That was not who I was expecting to open the door.

I said all I could think to say: "I'm here for the food."

He pushed the screen open.

"Come on in. Olga called to say you were on your way. It's here on the table."

I walked into the house, paused in the entryway and didn't want to go in any further. I noticed the strange lack of photos on the walls. Just a couple of fruit bowl still lifes, a framed museum exhibition poster.

"Are you house-sitting?" I asked. The question was dumb. It must have been. He looked at me as though I was dumb. But it felt like my brain was melting. Incapable of intelligent conversation. He grabbed a package on the table and held it out to me.

"I live here. You didn't know that? Olga is my wife."

"Oh." I took the food. "That's how Chelsea heard about . . . you were the one who'd mentioned the shelter to her."

His fingers slid across mine when we exchanged the bag. He stepped closer and smiled. Was he *flirting* with me?

"Chelsea had told me about the charity thing and I thought it would be a good idea to introduce her and Olga."

"Oh. Right." But why would Chelsea talk about out charity event to Professor Griffin? It didn't have much to do with chemistry. I couldn't recall ever discussing sorority news with my professors. It wasn't as though Chelsea and Griffin were close. She didn't mention him out of the context of classes. But then, maybe I was kidding myself. Maybe Chelsea didn't tell me everything, the way I used to think she did. Which meant Griffin could have been more to her than a teacher. A mentor. My gaze swept the room again. Taking in the array of tchotchkes on the mantle in the small living room. I began walking toward them. "Olga's last name is different than yours."

"Welcome to the twenty-first century, Katie."

"Right."

Professor Griffin waited, as though expecting another question, but I didn't have one coming. I thought about asking how he was doing, how his personal time was treating him, but it seemed too intimate. I wanted to tell him that I needed some personal time, too. Time to process. Time to grieve. It was so hard to mourn when I couldn't find closure for Chelsea's death. Not when the killer was still out there.

I planted myself in front of the fireplace. Looked at generic art prints, a book, a little soapstone elephant front and center.

I had an elephant just like that. So had Chelsea. An identical elephant, sold to us by a grinning woman in Tijuana last spring. Mine was green, but Chelsea had chosen a mottled red-orange. Just like the one on the mantle.

My breath quickened as I reached a hand to the elephant, my actions staggered. It couldn't be Chelsea's elephant. Despite those colors and that just right size and the way I could perfectly imagine her holding it in her hand and laughing.

"They're magical elephants," she'd said, winking at me under the brim of her floppy hat.

"How do you know?"

"The woman told me!"

"That's what I get for taking French instead of Spanish." I'd giggled. "What do they do?"

"Mine will bring me a lover."

"Ooo, nice. And mine?"

"Yours will keep hair from growing on your back."

The saleslady had laughed with us even though she'd had no idea what we were talking about.

Chelsea and her lover-elephant.

In Professor Griffin's house.

I drew my hand away before my fingers could touch the bauble. Ridiculous. There must have been a zillion elephants like this in L.A. Tourist baubles.

Griffin came next to me, placing his hand on my lower back, his fingers like ice on my skin. He gazed down at me, a smile tickling his mouth, his eyes predatory.

My hand bumped the elephant and sent it rattling to the floor.

"Sorry, Professor Griffin," I stuttered.

"Tod," he corrected, his fingers splayed on my back. "You were always one of my best students, Katie. One of the nicest I'd ever seen. So many friends."

"And then I lost my best friend."

He paused at that. I bent to retrieve the elephant. Griffin placed his hand over mine as I placed the carving on the mantle. "I'm sorry for your loss," he said.

The catch in his voice threw me off, a brief flicker of sadness brought lines across his forehead. He really did look sorry. And as cute as always. And like maybe he thought I needed . . . a kiss? . . . to feel better. I drew back slightly as his face closed in on mine.

My hands curled into fists. "Don't—"

The doorbell rang. Relief flooded by body. "That'll be Josh. He came with me."

I scurried out of the house, using every ounce of restraint I possessed to keep from flinging myself into Josh's arms. I looked over my shoulder as I crossed the lawn, shivering at the glint in Griffin's eyes.

18

I climbed into Josh's car and snapped the seatbelt in with shaky fingers.

"Was he hitting on you?" Josh said.

"You ask like that's the most incredible thing ever." My voice trembled. My body reeled, like I'd just gotten off a roller coaster.

"He's a professor."

"It's not unusual."

But I shuddered. A professor I once thought was so cute. Back when I thought his professor-authority was a barrier to the possibility that he could hit on a student. I don't know why I thought that. Student-professor relationships were common enough, right? It just never felt right to me. I had a line, even if no one else did. I didn't like knowing better, now. I still felt his fingers on my back, like cold pebbles.

"Could we go back to my house, please?"

"Let's drop off the food, then sure. We have time and the guys have everything ready."

"No! I mean, right now." I had to change out of these clothes. I had to get Griffin's lecherous look out of my head. I had to find my elephant, convince myself the one on the mantle couldn't have been Chelsea's.

"But the arena's on the way to the freeway."

"Screw the arena. The dog doesn't need the food right this moment." I squirmed, my shirt plastered to my back despite the air conditioned car. "I *need* to get home."

"What's going on?" We both watched as he drove past the arena.

I shook my head, surprised at my lack of control. This wasn't me. How could the advances of a too-forward professor shake me so badly? Because, maybe, it wasn't just me he'd been forward with.

Josh waited for me to spill, but I wasn't sure what to say.

The drive to Beverly Hills from the valley felt surprisingly short. Maybe it was the fog. Or the way that it felt as though I had only taken one breath from the moment we left the arena to the moment I found myself in my neighborhood.

"Tell me who you think killed Chelsea," Josh said as we pulled onto our street.

I stared at the manicured lawns out the window. I . . . wasn't sure I was right, anymore. "You'll think I'm crazy."

"Impossible. To think you're any more crazy than I already think you are." His eyes twinkled at me. I gave him a weak smile.

"It's just that he'd said anyone would want to get it from Chelsea." I dropped my voice, ashamed to say these things to Josh. To share something this personal. "And maybe Chelsea didn't tell me all her secrets, like I thought she did. What if they . . . And he's so strong," I rushed on. "He works out every day."

"Who?"

We neared my house. A familiar black shape flashed from the driveway. I clutched the door handle while Josh pulled to a stop in the street. We both hesitated, staring out the window at the tall figure waiting for us.

"Damon."

"Yeah, I see his car. What's he doing here?"

"I don't know," I choked, opening the door and falling out of Josh's car. I whispered the next words, imagining the way Damon would explode with anger if he heard the accusation, but needing Josh to know. "I think Damon's who killed Chelsea."

The briefest skepticism crossed Josh's face before it disappeared, before he decided to believe me. My shoes made a soft swishing noise against the grass as I crossed to Damon, raising my voice as I neared him. "What are you doing here?"

Damon leaned against his car, sunglasses dark as always. His mouth turned down when he saw Josh.

"What's he doing here?"

"She asked what *you're* doing here," Josh returned.

"I'm here to see my girlfriend's dad."

"I'm not your girlfriend anymore."

"Don't be like that. I came out here to plan a big graduation celebration for you. Show you how perfect we are for each other."

Next to me, Josh released an almost inaudible growl.

"Heel," I whispered. Then louder, to Damon: "You like showing girls how perfect you are, don't you?"

"Well, yeah. I'm a guy. Worked for you."

"Not just me, though," I said.

"You mean Stacey? Look, there is *nothing* there. I hoped you'd be a little jealous, sure. That seems to have worked, too." He held a hand to me. "Let's go inside and talk about it. You can go home, Hunter. This has nothing to do with you."

"He can stay. This is my house." I brushed aside Damon's hand. "And I didn't mean Stacey. I meant Chelsea."

Finally, Damon dropped the sunglasses off his face. Finally, he was going to tell me the truth. I braced myself for it, hardening my soul against the words that would cement his guilt.

And Chelsea's death.

His hands shook.

"Are you insane? What the hell does any of this have to do with Chelsea? She's *dead*."

"Watch it," Josh warned.

"Fuck off, Hunter." Damon stepped toward me, rage making him spit his words. "This is between me and Katie." He grabbed my wrist. I yanked it from him as Josh lunged forward. Damon pulled his arm back and decked Josh, connecting with the side of his head.

I yelped, shoving Damon, then danced back just as Josh leapt to his feet and plowed into Damon, knocking them both to the ground.

"Stop it!" I screamed, grabbing the back of Josh's shirt uselessly. My front door flew open and Dad marched across the lawn. He grabbed Josh's upper arm and tossed him behind his legs. Then he caught Damon mid-charge, his dress shoes slipping slightly on the slick grass, and shoved my ex-boyfriend toward his car.

"Not that I'm surprised boys are fighting over my daughter, but not in my yard. Get out of here, Damon, until you can control yourself. Josh, go home and get cleaned up."

The three of them eyed each other, Josh and Damon catching their breath. Blood trickled from Josh's nose. Damon sported a busted lip and an already swelling eye. But Dad's glare could turn the best of them inside out, standing there like he owned their souls. Damon stepped backwards, his eyes pasted on Josh in a warning, and slammed into his Corvette, peeling out of the driveway. Josh gave me a hooded look before crossing our yard to his. I listened for the slam of his front door, a way for him to tell me he was still mad at me, but the noise didn't come.

"Are you all right?" Dad wrapped an arm around my shoulders, his temperament fading into a gentleness he tended to reserve for me, only. I nodded into him. "Come inside."

"I will. I just want to make sure Josh is okay."

I twisted my shirt in my fingers as I walked to his house, my father's sigh following my progress to the yard over. My fingers pushed his door open and I called his name, waiting on the stoop for his reply. When had I become a stranger here? Was it that exact moment I'd told Josh I hated him for lying to me about everything being all right? The moment I told him to stay out of my life?

Josh didn't answer, but I let myself in, climbed the staircase, stood before his open bedroom door. Water ran in his bathroom. His grass-stained clothing lay on the floor in a heap next to the unmade bed.

I reached for his jeans, absently turning them right side out, picking up the paper that fell from one pocket, and sat on the edge of his bed.

The cops would have to be called. Damon . . . in handcuffs. His mom and dad not understanding, throwing money at their lawyers to keep him out of trouble, their reputations shattered, his brother losing his friends. They were decent people. Had always liked me. How could I do that to them? A silent tear rolled down my cheek. How could he have done this to *me*? And how could Chelsea have betrayed me?

I still couldn't believe she would do that. It wasn't possible.

Right?

I set Josh's jeans next to me and unfolded the paper. Olga's address. 2992 Belmont. Professor Griffin's hawk-gaze flashed in my head. And something else.

I knew that number.

I stood.

Oh my god.

I knew that number.

The water shut off.

But my mind worked overtime.

The elephant. And the address. And Mr. Griffin's hand on my back. And—

"What's wrong?"

Even Josh, muscular chest exposed and dripping hair next to me, heat and moisture coming off him in waves, couldn't tear me from remembering.

My subconscious must have formed the words, forced me to speak them, because I sure couldn't do it.

"Sigma is a type of covalent bond. Chelsea had been working with them for her final project."

Covalent bonds: a chemical bond characterized by the sharing of electrons. And Sigma was the strongest kind. Simply put, it was some serious attraction.

It could have been cute, had I not wanted to crawl in a hole and die.

Realization dawned on him as he read the numbers, went over them in his head. Converted names of months to numbers of months.

"Griffin killed her." He put his arms around me. His warm, wet arms and I didn't want to move ever again.

An incapacitating tidal wave of emotion threatened to take over the desperate numbness that froze my body. I had to move, to get out of here. I dropped the paper and clutched for the composure that swirled away from me like mist.

"We should go," I mumbled into Josh's chest. It was so hard to move my lips, my teeth.

"I'm not sure we should," he mumbled back.

"We have to." I went into auto-pilot. "We need to call the cops. And the show will be starting in a couple hours."

"Do you realize you're being ridiculous? Carolina can take over the project."

"No, she needs me. They all need me. Olga . . ." My heart thudded in my chest. What was I saying? I knew who killed my best friend and now I wanted to go work with his wife? Control slipped away from me to be replaced by the calmness of . . . madness. One quick movement and I would combust. "She's already so stressed and she doesn't even know what's going on and then we just don't show up and she freaks and at least I can help her with this because her life is about to fall apart. I'd know."

"You don't even know Olga."

"I don't have to know her to know that what's coming is going to destroy her. It would destroy anyone. It's destroying me."

Josh sighed and I knew I'd won.

But neither of us moved. Finally, I reached for my cell. "I have to call Charlie." My voice was too shaky. It gave everything away. I cleared my throat and dialed.

"Katie?" he answered. "Is everything okay? What's going on? Are you calling about Bryant? Was there something on his cell phone?"

"I figured out Sigma2992," I said, deciding I wouldn't beat around the bush. I tried so dang hard to keep my voice steady but it shook anyway. There was silence on the line after my announcement. "Charlie?"

"I'm here," he said. He paused. "It's not—? Do I want to know?"

I closed my eyes. I wished now that I didn't know.

"Sigma2992 isn't a frat and a birth date. It's a code. A kind of bond. From chemistry. And an address. In the valley. It's where—" I took a deep breath and tried to not rush out the information. "It's where Tod Griffin lives. Our chemistry professor. Mine and Chelsea's."

Silence.

"Charlie?"

"I'm here."

Silence.

"That's the classroom where."

"Yes."

Silence.

Then a sob.

"Oh god."

"Charlie," I whispered.

"How did you find out?"

"I'm working on this charity thing. With his wife."

"His wife? Oh god."

"She asked me to pick something up from her house. And there he was. Being all creepy. And then I saw the address. And everything hit me."

Sob.

"You really think it's him?"

I scratched the polish off my fingernail because that was the only thing that focused me, kept me from screaming.

"I don't know. The janitor. Just because they were . . . doesn't mean he—" He couldn't have. There had to be . . . something. Yes, let it be the frat guy. Some pathetic creep that I would never have to see again. Please. But I knew better. "Who else could have?"

I couldn't see Charlie, but I could tell he was nodding. Maybe I could hear it. He sniffed, calmed himself.

"Okay. I'm going to call the police now."

I nodded.

"Okay."

"Okay."

We still held onto our phones. It was more than a landline. It was a lifeline.

"Do you want me to call you after?"

Yes. No. God no.

"I have to head back to the arena in a minute. I can't leave the ladies hanging. Or Olga."

"Olga's the wife?"

"Yeah."

"Oh god."

"Yeah."

"Maybe you shouldn't go back. It's a lot to ask."

"She doesn't even know. I have to just be normal."

"I'll call your cell when I know something."

"Okay."

"Katie?"

"Yes?"

"I love you, honey."

"Love you, too, Charlie."

I pressed the end call button and set the phone down.

"He's calling the police?" Josh asked from behind me.

"Yes." I fought the urge to settle back in his embrace. "How long do you think before Olga finds out?"

"Too soon."

I considered that and shuddered.

"I still don't think it's a good idea to go back."

"I know." I loved that Josh was so worried about me, but if there was a chance I could give Olga a few moments of peace before her world falls apart I was taking it. It wasn't fair, what happened to Chelsea. Not fair to me and not fair to her.

With a sigh, I opened my texts and scrolled through my contacts, my thumb pausing over my ex-boyfriend's name.

"What are you doing?"

"I treated him . . . so badly," I said, pressing the letters that would form my apology. *I'm sorry*, I typed. *I know who did it.*

We drove back to the arena in silence. Not even music to drown out our thoughts. I wondered what Josh was thinking, wondered if both of our heads were swimming, drowning, with thoughts about us, about Mr. Griffin and Olga, about Chelsea. I wanted to kiss him as he drove, over and over again. Connect with someone who was here, who was real, who grounded me. Cause an accident. Stop the earth from spinning. But I thought of Olga. Would one of us slip up in front of her and leak the information we had? Did we even want to have to face her at all? I knew I didn't.

We got to the arena way too quickly. Even the time it took to find parking in the crowded lot was too quick. Josh cut the engine and took my hand and we sat in the silence until he leaned over and took my face in his hands.

"Stay close to me," he said.

The arena was crowded and I waited outside while Josh poked in to see if Olga was there. I wandered further down the hallway, on the lookout for Olga, pausing to stroke the silky back of a mutt that Courtney Dreger was taking for a walk. A few steps beyond, a hallway branched off the main one and I took it, grateful for the quiet. I took a left at another hallway and stopped.

There she was.

"Olga," I said. I cleared my throat. "Um, we're back. With the food."

She didn't look at me, just continued unloading the last of the dog crates from a small cart onto the floor, then set a bottle of cleaning solution and a few rags next to them. I fidgeted uncomfortably. I didn't think she had ever really liked me. Maybe I should've just gone to get Josh. Maybe I shouldn't have walked away from him in the first place.

I spun around to leave but she stopped me with her words.

"I didn't think you'd be back. But since you are, can you wipe down these crates? We're trying to head off a sickness that's spreading amongst the dogs."

I took the rag she offered me. "Why didn't you think I'd be back?"

She made a few notes on a clipboard. Set it down and reached for her medicine case. She opened it and, inside, I saw a lining of black satin under a myriad of tools and medicines. Under the lid, a row of tiny bottles with silver caps gleamed at me, winked at me. "Chelsea had mentioned you to me. When we first met. After you'd left, I realized you didn't know who my husband was. But I'm sure you knew everything else about him. And her. Since you two were so close."

My heart dropped. Had he called her back after I'd left? A last ditch effort to come clean? I avoided looking at her because, in the end, I guess we weren't that close. Chelsea hadn't trusted me with her secrets.

"I didn't know. Even though she was my best friend," I said. The words sounded far away. Eaten up by the hallway.

"That must have been hard. To lose her."

I didn't get it. Did she want to, I don't know, *bond* over our shared misery?

"It was," I said. "It is."

I didn't know what else to say. What the heck does one say to the wife of the guy your best friend was having an affair with? "I'm so sorry . . . about what they . . . about what happened to you."

She stared at me, one eyebrow cocked. "I see," she whispered. "You don't know everything, do you?"

I sunk onto a large crate and looked blurrily down at my hands, folded in my lap around the rag.

"What don't I know?" I whisper.

"Katie, this has all been dealt with. We're trying to move on, my husband and I. I knew about their relationship almost from the beginning."

"How?"

She sighed. "Our marriage is open."

"Open?" I knew what it meant. I thought. But I didn't know what it meant for Chelsea.

"Yes, open. He may see other people and I may see other people. It's not the sort of thing that works for everyone, but it does for us."

"He wasn't cheating on you?"

"No."

So she knew about everything. The affair, that wasn't actually an affair because it was okay in their open relationship. But what about the baby? Professor Griffin's plans to leave?

How he killed her?

I felt dizzy and nauseous, sitting in this woman's presence, dread and realization crashing over me at the same moment, seizing my breath, halting the precious flow of oxygen to my brain. She had known. The whole time. Her life ready to collapse around her.

Professor Griffin was creepy, but a killer?

He wasn't the only one with so much to lose. Even open marriages don't leave much room for a baby.

Was Olga a killer?

I clasped the sides of the crate to keep from toppling onto the floor, to keep from leaping to my feet and dashing away. She would follow me, she would do the same thing to me that she did to Chelsea. How could I not have seen it? All this time, working under his wife's nose.

"But what did you do . . . " My voice cracked. " . . . when you found out about the pregnancy?"

Olga ignored the question, pulled bottles of medicine from the medicine case, counted them and made more notes on her clipboard. Then she picked up a syringe topped with the kind of needle you only see in horror films. She jammed it into one of the bottles from her case and pulled back on the plunger. We both watched as the liquid bubbled up inside the container. She set the first bottle in the case and picked up another one.

"Two," I said, wearily.

"There's a virus that needs taken care of. Have to be careful, though. This stuff is potent. Could kill a person."

I closed my eyes. *Virus*. What a strange thing to call Chelsea, to call me. *She* was the one who said it was okay for her husband to sleep with other people. I looked around, towards the staircase, on the ground, at the silvery shine of the top corner of my phone poking out of my bag. Where was Josh?

"I have to make a call." Her hand reached my arm just as my fingers curled around my purse handles.

"Wait, Katie." She furrowed an eyebrow at me, a maneuver that was so innocent, so questioningly dog-like that I had to look away to keep from being taken in by false claims of innocence. How slowly did this scene have to go before she would be convinced of the lie that I suspected nothing? "I'm sorry you found out about . . . them this way. To answer your question, yeah, the pregnancy made things . . . different. Difficult. It had to be dealt with . . . Katie? You look pale. Do you want something to eat?"

She stood there, slightly hunched over, holding that full syringe in the air like a talisman, a threat, a promise. Could I get away faster than she could inject me? I inhaled slowly, so slowly because it hurt, and pasted on a smile.

"I should go."

"I have some nuts in my bag—"

"You're crazy!" I didn't mean to blurt out the desperation at the forefront of my mind. The air between us seized, particles freezing with expectation and fear. No, she wasn't the crazy one. I was. Accusing everyone with only the slightest provocation when really . . . more than anything . . . *I just didn't want my best friend dead at all.*

I ran. Olga sputtered behind me, but I couldn't make out a word she said as I whipped around the corner, down the hall and slammed into a set of broad shoulders.

"Katie?"

"Damon." The relief of a familiar face and voice sent my breath from my lungs in an emphatic whoosh. "Get me out of here."

"I heard you scream. I'll take care of you."

He gripped my hand tightly and led me down another dark hallway.

"I need to find Josh."

"He's down here. Doing stuff with the breakers." Damon pushed aside a few brooms to clear the path for a door. He turned the handle slowly, silently, then we both stepped into the dark space beyond. I clutched his hand with a tremble and took another step backwards, but my shoe found no ground to settle upon. I tipped at the top of the stairs and reached for Damon to right my balance. He moved a hand to my chest, grasped my arm and stared me full in the face, one quiet, stony moment between us, and pushed.

19

I screamed, abruptly cutting the sounds off as the air was knocked out of my lungs. I tumbled down the stairs to the sounds of a clanging, smashing, and cracking symphony, landing on the side of my face in a heap on the concrete floor below, the impact rupturing my nose and splattering my clothes with blood. I heard the door above me close, the streaking, ingratiating sounds of objects being dragged in front of it, and reached for the bottom step.

I cried out in pain. Stabbing pain that tore through my sides and out my shoulders. I flopped back on the floor and gasped in the aged, dusty air. It was hard to breathe. So hard to get oxygen to my brain, to be able to still myself long enough to understand what had just happened. I sucked in sharp little bits of air while my lungs protested every movement, struggled against the pain, against the bright flashes of light that obscured my vision. I reached into my pocket and pulled out my phone to dial Josh.

He picked up on the first ring, his voice worried, frantic.

"Where are you?"

I gasped, fought the pain, gasped, sucked in the dirt on the concrete next to my mouth. I choked on it, on blood.

"Where are you!"

There was so much in my throat blocking my words: tears and blood and filth and the need to keep the passageway open for the tiny amount of air I could get through. I heard him running, searching rooms, all through the phone.

"Under," I rasped.

"Katie! Under what!"

"He said . . . where the breakers are."

I searched the room, locked eyes with dark, shadowy objects, listened to the echo of sound from somewhere, everywhere above me.

Some distance away I saw the outline of a crate. A big, old-fashioned wooden crate. I reached out to it, letting my hand fall to the ground, grasped the concrete, and pulled myself toward it.

I squealed from the pain.

I could hear Josh on the phone still. Talking, talking. The sound grew fuzzier the closer I got to the crate. I can't hear you, I said. But I think I didn't actually say it aloud. Only in my head.

He said my name. Again and again. I heard that much. I could make out that word no matter how or where he said it.

The crate was right there. Right in front of me. I eased myself around behind it and rested against it. It would be harder for him to find me here. When he came back. I knew he would come back. I tried to slow my breathing, but couldn't. I just wasn't getting enough air. Everything was quiet. Quiet and dark. I thought, then, that the phone had gone silent. But it hadn't. It was just me.

#

"Hey, girl."

I danced across a wildflower strewn meadow and flung myself into her outstretched arms. We hugged and skipped and laughed and the sun shone down on us. We flopped onto the ground and she chose a long piece of grass and plucked it and stuck it in her mouth and I picked daisies and began braiding them into a headpiece.

The breeze was soft around us. It lifted pieces of our hair and flung them into our eyes, our mouths. We laughed as we brushed them away. When the crown was finished I fitted it on Chelsea's head and she stood and strutted around for me like a queen and tossed her skirts to and fro and I laughed at her struts and called her names, silly, too-young-for-us names like duchess and spoiled brat. And she stuck her tongue out at me and I couldn't stop laughing. We had so much fun.

I fell back into the grass and my ribs hurt. From all that laughing.

"Oh Chels, I miss you."

She knelt down next to me and pulled my shirt up to expose my mid-section and blew a raspberry on my belly. And it hurt to keep laughing. But I laughed anyway, so remarkably free. Chelsea flopped to the ground beside me and filled her lungs with air and I was jealous for that.

"It gets better, K," she said to the sky.

I followed her gaze upward and watched as a flock of birds passed us overhead in perfect triangle formation. Like a pyramid.

"When you're dead?"

One of the birds from the back row tipped its head down and looked at us, slowing its flight speed and breaking formation. When it realized we were nothing interesting, it beat its wings again, urgently, to catch up with the flock and settle into its position again.

Chelsea rolled onto her side and propped her head on her hand. She studied me briefly before rolling her eyes at me.

"That's not what I meant. I meant when you deal with it, all of it, it gets better." She still chewed on her grass. The daisies sunk into her glossy hair. She was a goddess. The goddess of the meadow. "And now you'll learn what happened to me. And you'll be able to let it go. It's what I want you to do. Promise me you'll let it go, K."

I closed my eyes against the sun because staring at it blinded me. I stretched my arms and legs out into the grasses and wildflowers, brushing them aside, like I was going to make a snow angel, and ignored the shot of pain in my sides as I moved. It was peaceful here. There were green and violet and black butterflies and fat buzzing bumblebees. And freshness in the air and warmth on my face. I ignored Chelsea's question because I couldn't feel the right answer yet. Right now, the whys and hows overwhelmed everything else. But I would. Eventually. I knew I would.

"You were running from it, too," I said. "Running from him. Both of them?"

"But you understand why," she said and I didn't have to nod for her to know that I agreed with her.

I knew why. She wanted to go away, escape so she could process things. And she wanted to take me with her. A year in Europe. Or wherever. Wherever I wanted to go, anywhere I would have gone would have been fine with her. Just so long as we got away. From everyone. We both had things to run from. I wished I knew if she would have kept the baby. I wished I knew if there was really something between her and Damon, if she could actually have done that to me. If the best friend I'd opened myself fully to—who didn't reciprocate—could possibly have done something so horrible to me. But impossibilities were better laid to rest as such, retaining the friend I knew—what I knew of her—more important that contemplating the ifs. And maybe, maybe, I didn't really want to know.

"But you figured it all out anyway," she said, twisting a fat Bluebell stem between her fingers. "Smart girl."

I snorted. I hadn't figured anything out. I took all the wrong steps. Everything I knew, everything I was, I had stumbled upon. Lucky, maybe. But not smart.

"Not smart enough to avoid ending up here."

Chelsea laughed.

"And where is here, do you think?"

I gazed at my best friend. What kind of question was that?

"If you're here it must be heaven." I looked around me, taking my time, taking in the serenity. "Although I'd kind of thought heaven would be different. A beach maybe. New York City?"

Chelsea laughed again. I admired her white teeth, the way she smiled so freely. And so honestly.

"And Simon will come, too, won't he? He'll be here soon. To welcome me. I can't wait to see him, you know. It's been so, so long. And I've loved him so, so much. All this time."

Chelsea moved in close and put her hand on the side of my face.

"Oh, Katie," she smiled. Her eyes were sad. "This is just a dream."

She patted my face.

Hard.

"Katie."

A slap.

"Katie."

After the light of the meadow and the sparkling rays of the sun, the blackness I awoke to was even darker than before. I felt a shock of fear that I was blind. Or that heaven wasn't for me after all.

Another slap.

A moan.

"You're awake," he whispered. Then he moved closer to press his lips against where his palm had connected with my face. "I'm so sorry, I didn't mean to hurt you. I was worried you would never wake up."

I came to slowly, much slower than I knew I should but I couldn't seem to speed up the process. My vision adjusted to the black. My head pounded. It hurt to breathe, but my breathing was so shallow that I hardly felt it. My face ached, right in the middle.

I was no longer sprawled on the floor behind the wooden crate, but propped up against it, back straight, head lolling.

"You thought you would get away with it," I mumbled. "Blame it on the janitor. Or Griffin. That's why . . . the chem lab closet. You were there that morning." So strong, to have fetched her from water, to heave Chelsea into the closet. To hoist me up when I had been nothing but dead weight.

He made a face, a scrunched-mouth-to-the-side face, a loss-of-patience, look-to-the-ceiling-for-help face, and waved his arms around, his fist clenched around a butcher knife. I wanted to laugh at his slash film weapon, but it hurt so much.

"I don't care about them. They're nothing. I don't . . . I don't even want to have to be here," he said, exasperated. "I don't want to have to explain things to you, as though I did something wrong. Because I didn't. It was an accident. I pushed her in the pool, but it was playful. Playing around. Understand?" He gave me an earnest look and I didn't care how sincere he was or sorry he was, the only thing I could really see was that knife, swerving and switching through the air like a car spinning into an accident.

"Yes," I choked out, desperate for the words to come out stronger, to not whimper. Chelsea had been too drunk to swim and he'd pushed her in. But no . . . if Chelsea was pregnant she wouldn't have been drinking. Did no one notice him holding her under, the way he'd had to? Did they assume he was carrying her off to do . . . something horrible? They probably *cheered* him on. Scoring with his girlfriend's best friend.

But no one would have told the police? It was dark at that party. There was a lot of alcohol. Hard to remember who was with who, in the end.

But then he put Chelsea in that closet.

"Oh God, Katie. Oh God, that means so much. You don't even know. It's not like I was into her. A little bit of slumming maybe . . . just a little thrill . . . I had your face in my mind the whole time. Even if I was thinking about her, I was picturing you, it was really you. You were always there, always the one."

I nodded dazedly, not sure he could see me, but the lilting action of head back and forward gave me something to focus on while his stuttered words tore at me like a second weapon.

He stood quickly and circled my chair. "It was only that one time. We'd had too much to drink. We made a mistake. But she wanted to tell you. I couldn't let that happen. You would have lost your best friend and your boyfriend all at once."

I was desperate to close my eyes but I knew that the moment I looked away was the moment he would attack me.

"It was an accident," he repeated. "She fell in the pool. We were too drunk, remember? I tried to help her out . . . I think . . . she was struggling so much . . . I could hardly look at her after what we'd done. I was so sorry for it."

I shook my head, my jawbone slapping against the cold metal, feeling the sharpness of it in my teeth, the pain of it in the back of my neck.

"You watched her drown?" I closed my eyes, but the vision that greeted my attempted respite was her face, every orifice open wide, screaming soundless, bursting bubbles, flailing her arms and legs and nobody realizing she was drowning, not dancing. She was a great swimmer. She swam every morning. Damon's excuses, his lies, swirled like a carnival ride. And made me just as sick. "You put her in the closet?"

"Don't cry," he whispered, reaching up to wipe away a tear rolling down my cheeks. "It wasn't your fault."

"It was yours," I whispered, not caring that one false word and he could slit my throat because, suddenly, I knew Josh was there. He was near, I could feel it.

"Katie. You don't know how sorry I am over all of this."

Did people get a sense of lucidity just before they were about to die, know the way I knew that they were going to be saved, or was that the conundrum here: lucidity over being saved because I knew I was going to die? I wondered what Chelsea had thought about right before she died, whether someone would come in and save her. If she worried about losing her best friend because she'd cheated with Damon.

No, I thought now. That wouldn't have ended us. But then, at this point, I would let anything go if it meant I could have her back. I loved her. Still did. No one who loved her was near as she inhaled the water. Not like they are near to me. They needed to know where I was.

I inhaled and screamed, right through Damon's breaking my skin with the knife, right through his sad, apologizing smile. The cut, between my neck and shoulder, pierced me on an elemental level as the steel of the weapon reacted with the metal in my blood. It was cold and burning at the same time, despairing even as it was non-fatal, a threat, only.

He wanted to stop, even I could tell that by the way his body started shaking, by the way his eyes flitted back and forth, searching for a way out, so scared, so confused, but instead he pressed again, harder, closer to my throat when the shouts from upstairs became louder than my own gargled grunts, when things slammed and something heavy and solid flew at Damon's shoulder and knocked him to the ground. When the shadows gathered around me and worked at the duct tape holding me to the crate. Even when I looked down to my wrist, to the place where my palm was at an odd, unnatural angle with my forearm, even when the fierce pain of the cuts on my neck thumped, as though my heart was pumping blood, life, directly out of those slashes, I did not scream.

Two tall shadows moved to Damon's fallen body, inspected him, and bound his own limbs together. A third figure finished removing the tape from my ankles and moved onto the tape on my wrists. He worked slowly and quickly at the same time and his fingers shook. He looked me in the eyes.

"The police are on their way. And an ambulance." His voice was choked and uncertain. He tugged gently at the tape once he had reached the last layer, the one stuck to my skin, pulling at my pale hairs. It wouldn't hurt, I wanted to tell him. Just rip it off. Nothing could possibly hurt me now.

It did hurt, as he pulled it off. Despite the pains in my chest and the blood caking beneath my nose and chin and the ugly set of my wrist, the tape coming off did hurt. But I did not scream. I would be brave, because he was here and there was nothing to be afraid of.

I tried to be fearless.

"I'm an idiot, Josh."

But when my bonds were free and my arms dropped to the side, blood dripping down into them, bringing them to life again, and Josh reached for me and gathered me in his arms and lifted me, crushing my ribs to him, then, I couldn't help it. The pain flashed through me like a strobe light at a disco. My eyes bulged. I screamed.

20

Everyone came to see me while I was in the hospital.

Dad came. *You'll be okay.*

Mrs. Mathis came and cried and cried.

Professor Griffin came. *I'm so sorry*, I said to him. *I was so wrong.* But he squeezed my hand anyway and said he was the one who needed to apologize.

Olga who, despite my suspicion, was researching a new virus that was sweeping through the shelter dog population and was trying to heal them with her medicine. She told me she had wanted to help Chelsea in any way she could. That she was happy to help raise the baby, give Chelsea money, anything. I told her she was an inspiration to me.

And then there was this shadow that came when it was dark out and laced his fingers with mine and moved in so close that I could feel his breath on my ear and smell the perfect scent of him. I had so much to say to him, but he always came when I was mostly asleep, as though he'd rather not hear what I had to say.

My mom never came. Maybe I wasn't sick enough for her, but maybe the truth was that she was too sick for me.

My body felt good as new when they released me. Just a bit of a lingering dull pain in my wrist and sides. But the bruising on my face was gone and bandages covered the rest. A fast healer, the nurses had said, like it was a great accomplishment. If they could see inside, though, at how long I'd held onto open wounds, they'd never have let me out.

My sorority sisters had attended my classes, laptops in hand, so I could keep up with studies virtually. I loved them hard for their efforts. I studied whenever I was alone and there was nothing left to do after release. Now, I ached to keep busy. Do something with this body that had taken a few weeks to feel like mine again.

I stood at the edge of my pool, needing my limbs, alive and free, to move. Something had to move. If my thoughts did I would realize Chelsea was really, truly dead. Allowed to die by someone I had once cared about, had once trusted. But that was what I needed. I feared the bitter emptiness in my chest, threatening to overwhelm me with that truth.

So I slipped in, trying to face my fear of drowning.

The water was perfect. It was always perfect. It swirled around me and soothed me and encouraged me to relax and let go. I listened to the water, let it tell me what to do and what not to do, sinking in and under its embrace. My hair danced around my face, partnered up with the water, and they tangoed with each other.

It was all over. And it wasn't Griffin or Olga or the janitor or the poor frat boy. Poor guy. Charlie had scared him, even if Charlie was too sweet to have done anything really horrible. But hate changed people.

Understanding did, too, but now I needed to accept that I would have to live without that. Maybe Chelsea was worried I would despise her because of one mistake, because my perfect boyfriend in my perfect life wasn't as seamless as I'd thought it was. Maybe it was all about protection: protecting me, protecting herself. Maybe she was scared, intimidated by the way I'd planned every last piece of my life. Uncertain if I would be there for her if her plans got in the way of mine.

Of course I would have been.

I knew I should go up for air. What a luxury it was to breathe, to live.

But my arms didn't want to move. It felt so good to be supported weightless and thoughtless in this semi-darkness. It was beautiful and still and silent here. I thought, maybe, I'd stay. Just for a little while, just long enough to understand what Chelsea went through. Just long enough to feel content with the world again.

There was a disturbance, and the sound, when it finally reached me through the thick warm water of the pool, was heavy and muted. I knew that sound traveled more slowly through water than through air. The motion of the water from that something or someone swayed me from side to side like a Hawaiian hula dancer figurine, with their draping grass skirts and their coconut shell bras, the motion measured and baseless. I was surprised at how quickly the shadow form reached me, how much faster than the sound he was as he dove for me and grasped out to me, latched onto me with his hands, with his strength.

He yanked me out the of the water so forcefully that my eyes closed against the friction and when I took that first breath of warm air I didn't want to open them again right away.

He muttered over me.

"Oh, Katie, oh, no, no, no," he whispered. "Please, no, please." He took my face in his hands and I suspected what he was going to do next and, despite everything I've done and every meanness I've been to him, I wanted him to do it. I wanted him to press his lips against mine and trade his life giving breath with my own deadness. I wanted to breathe back into him so that we could be one. So that he could save me and I could stop pretending I hated him.

But I couldn't deceive him anymore.

I opened my eyes and looked at him, his mouth creased with worry and tension and wanting me to live. Hope crossed his face when I opened my eyes, and he pulled back, just a little.

"I wasn't trying to kill myself," I whispered. "I wasn't drowning. Not in the water, at least. Elsewhere, everywhere else, yes. Everywhere you're not I find myself drowning. But not in the pool. Not today. I tried to stay away from you, but I couldn't. I always went back. How could I stay away from you? Not when I feel like this."

And the thing I wanted him most to do, he did. He lifted my body up to meet him and pressed his lips against mine in a kiss that freed worry and anger and hatred, but had room for things that were so much better. His arms tightened around me, his kiss deepened and I met him with a force of my own, our collision tasting like heaven. I buried my hand in his hair, pulling him against me harder, needing him to cover every inch of me. My thoughts fell away as the feel of Josh filled my mind. As my body roared to life. He tasted like pool water and Lucky Charms, a combination that only worked with him. Josh stopped and pulled back, just an inch, breathless, kissed my lips a second time, softly, then my chin and my lips again, then he pulled me closer and let me press my cold wet nose into his chest and he kissed the top of my head.

"I wanted to let you give me mouth to mouth," I said.

He laughed. A rumbling, comforting thing to feel and then hear.

"I didn't want to have to do that. I didn't want that to be necessary. This was far, far better."

We were silent for several moments and I let the memory of a girl with thick, dark hair and playful eyes wash over me. She was gone, really gone, and I would never have another moment with her. The realization was almost too much to take; I needed her light and her smarts and her confidence in me but now there was nothing but a void in my heart that felt too big to heal. What would I do without her? My Chelsea. My crazy best friend. I suffocated under the emotion: the loss of a friendship that ended too early and the anger for the plans she had but would never live out. I closed my eyes and pictured her face and heard her laugh ringing in my ears, and tried to quell the hatred for the one who took her from me because she was gone and she shouldn't be.

Josh pressed his face in my hair.

"I came to check on you. At the right time, I think. What were you doing in there?"

It was hard for him to ask. Hard for him to expect an answer. And I knew why. I had demeaned him for so long, devalued everything he was to me for so long that he couldn't possibly trust me anymore. It had been years since we'd said anything meaningful to each other, and now he had to wonder, did one kiss mean we were childhood friends again?

He rubbed my arm as I thought about it. Childhood friends? Perhaps not. Perhaps now it was time to move to something else, on to something better.

"I was thinking. I wasn't trying to drown myself, promise, but I *was* wondering what it was like to drown. I was wondering what it was like for Chelsea. All of it." My voice shook. I hardly realized it but I was talking through a torrent of tears that I couldn't get to stop if my life depended on it. But it felt good to let this go.

"What it was like when she found out she was pregnant and whether she was scared about it or angry or happy. What it was like when she told Griffin—if she wanted to tell him at all or if he just found out. And then she just fell out of that closet. And we all saw it happen. What was he thinking? Josh, I just want to hate him so much because so much of it was his fault and he's a horrible person, but I don't hate him for some reason. I should. I want to. His e-mails said he loved her." I paused to catch my breath but the tears kept coming and my voice was halting and catching. "And, and, what about me? Cause I loved her, too. And I miss her. I told her everything—about Simon and my mom. But she didn't tell me. Why did she think I was a terrible friend? That hurts. Being under the water as long as I was hurt, too. So it must have hurt her. What was she thinking when it happened? How hard did she fight to get to the surface? Was she thinking about the baby while she . . . ? Oh god, she couldn't have been drunk. Not if she knew she was pregnant. She would never do that. He must have . . . Oh, god."

"The police will know that. They'll take care of that, promise." Josh let me wipe my snot across the front of his shirt. God, it was good to be in his arms again.

"I've come to a realization," I said. "I don't want to live like this anymore, like some suitcase stuffed with dark, cobwebby memories. I want to be able to think about Simon because I haven't let myself think about him since he died. And I loved him so much and I want him back because he was taken from me way too soon. And I want to forgive my mother for abandoning me when I really needed her, and I even want her to forgive herself for not saving Simon because I think I did a long time ago. And I want to tell my dad thank you for sticking with me when mom left and my stepmom left, and even though we're both so busy, doing little things to remind me that we're on the same side.

"I want to see Chelsea again, and talk to her and paint her toenails for her and dance naked in fountains with her and watch her argue with Charlie and win 'cause she always did because she was so damn smart and she just cared about every single thing there was to care about, even me. And I want to be your friend again. I really do. I want to eat Lucky Charms with you and go over to your house every day like I used to and fight with you and make up with you and love you even when I'm sure I hate you.

"I love you, Josh." The sobs racked my body now, as I sank into my admission. "I loved you when you were my best friend in the whole world, and I love you now, when I want to be your best friend in the whole world. I love that you've stuck by me and I love that you've never just let me be, even when I wanted you to. You've always been the one. I wish I'd never let myself forget that. And I'm sorry, Josh, for being so horrible to you all these years when, really," and now I made myself look at him even though I was sure I looked an absolute wreck, "really, all I did was love you."

And Josh melted. His eyes got all liquid and shadowy and his arms tightened around me. His breath softened until it was almost nothing. He brushed my wet hair back and cupped my face in his hands and kissed me, gentle as a whisper. He held me there for a while, even after he had pulled his lips back. I opened my eyes. His were still closed. He was beautiful.

I didn't want to ask because he couldn't possibly, not after the way I had treated him, but I had to know anyway.

"Do you love me?" I whispered.

And I knew it before he spoke it. I should have known it all along. He was always showing me.

"Of course I do. I always loved you."

I shivered.

He scooped me up and carried me upstairs, setting me on my bed before entering my closet and emerging with my pile of clothes from earlier. He set the clothes on my bed and went to the door, pausing with his hand on the doorknob.

"I'll be just outside. You should get dressed. So you don't get sick."

Didn't he realize how sick I already was? He saw everything.

He moved to close the door, but I beat him to it. In a single-minded rush I grabbed the edge of the door and flung it open and pulled him back inside.

"Stay." I wrapped my arms around his waist. "Stay with me."

It wasn't a perfect moment. It was just me and the boy next door and our shared history in my bedroom. And I was all snotty and red-eyed. But that was exactly what I wanted. Someone who knew everything there was to know about me and loved me still. I slid my hands under his shirt and felt his hot skin against my palms.

"Katie," he whispered. And there was a warning sound to his voice.

I ignored him. I knew what he wanted to say, so much for us to talk about and a million things to say, but all I wanted was to press my skin against his and feel our shared heat. All I wanted was what I'd once known of him, had always known of him. The familiarity, the memories coming to life again.

I lifted his shirt, slowly, and pressed my lips to where my hands had been. He smelled so good, like love and honesty and home.

I tugged his shirt up further, silently demanding him to raise his arms. I worried briefly that he might resist, might fight me on this. For my own good. But he didn't. He lifted his arms and let me undress him. And when his chest and his arms were no longer clothed, he swallowed nervously. And touched my face. And lifted my chin to him and kissed me again.

Maybe he did understand. Maybe he needed me right now as much as I needed him. Our lips met gently, searching. Deciding if it was as good, as perfect as it had once been. I caught his bottom lip between my teeth and tugged playfully. His mouth turned up in response and he slid his tongue across my lips, slowly tasting me. Shivers began in the back of my neck, crawled down my spine, building a steady fire throughout my body.

"Katie," he whispered, and this time there was no warning, no hesitation, just wanting and needing and certainty. We were Katie and Josh again, ready to explore. Ready to offer everything we are to one another. With Josh, I was complete.

I put my arms around his neck and he swept me off my feet and carried me to my bed again and set me on the edge again.

He knelt before me and kissed my legs, beginning with my ankles, first one, and then the other. He set my body to a slow burn, and I wanted him more than I'd wanted anything in my life, but he was deliberate and purposeful as though he'd planned for this moment forever and he wasn't giving in to anything but his own plans.

Intensity grew across my skin, in my belly, between my legs. My body began to throb gently, in time to my deep, quickening breathing.

I watched the top of his head as he touched me, and I filled to bursting with how much I loved him and how sad I was that I ever let that fade and how glad I was that he hadn't given up on me. He stroked the insides of my thighs as lightly as a feather, then followed that up with his lips, dragging them across my skin or dotting playful kisses like butterflies. Like the fluttering in my stomach and chest.

He moved higher, skipping over the part of my body that craved his touch the most, and drew circles across my belly with his tongue.

"You taste so good," he said. "You taste like I remember."

And that's exactly what I wanted. To go back to what we were, to bring that into our now, into our future. I took his hands and cupped them around my breasts, showing him how I liked to be touched, letting him take over as his thumbs rounded on my nipples, hardening with wanting him. He put his mouth over them. I arched my back under the sensation, like bolts of lightning across my body, into my ribs and down my legs.

"Josh," I moaned. "I'm yours."

He stood and lifted my hand and pressed his lips to where the cast let air touch my palm.

I scooted back on the bed and pulled him down to me and kissed him as he settled in next to me. I undressed the rest of him slowly, following my fingers with my lips, with a memory flaring more and more into dazzled light with each inch I uncovered. That lightly salty line down the center of his stomach. That scar on his elbow. The rise and fall of his knees. And then he undressed me slowly, too, and kissed my skin as though he worshipped it. Did he remember, too? How perfect this always had been, how perfect it was, now? How two people could find each other again after years, too many lost years?

When he slid back up to me, our noses almost touching, I stared into his hazel eyes, dark with passion, and saw it. The way he felt the same as I did. The rightness of us coming back together.

He edged on top of me and placed his fingers and palms around my hips, never breaking eye contact. I lost my breath when our bodies met, when he entered me, feeling him outside and inside me. Engulfed by him in the loveliest way. I pressed my shoulders against his pillows and met him movement for movement. And then I took control, pushing him gently aside and climbing atop. His firmness and his hands and his mouth rubbed against every part of my body and I leaned down to kiss him and the sky seemed to open above us and it was all I could do to keep control over our rhythm when, really, I wanted to let my limbs loosen, fall, swim, drown in the sea of him.

As our power built, Josh raised himself into sitting position and I flung my arms around his head and shoulders and he buried his face in my breasts and dug his fingertips into my back and when I burst, I flung my head back so that my hair was like flame and he brought me back to him and covered my mouth with his, searching and promising, as our bodies shuddered together.

And afterwards he stayed with me and whispered over and over how he loved me. And I closed my eyes and listened to his voice and his breath and I kissed his shoulder and told him I loved him and tried to pretend that my hair wasn't drying into some hideously funky Medusa shape.

#

I slept a little. A hard, dark, dreamless sleep like I hadn't had in so long. And if it had been anything besides Josh's kisses on my temple waking me, I would have fought waking. But I remembered where I was and who I was with and I snuggled into him with a smile and a sigh.

"Hi," I whispered.

I felt his mouth, against my head, form up into a smile.

"How long was I asleep?"

"Mmm, about an hour."

"Is that all? It felt longer."

"I liked watching you. It reminded me of when you used to sleep over. When we were younger."

"You watched me sleep back then?"

"I watched you all the time."

"Creepy."

He chuckled. "In a not creepy, sad puppy dog jilted boy next door way." Then he sobered. "I watched you dive into the pool. You never came back up."

We held silent for several minutes after that. How could I explain it to him? I didn't know right then, but, eventually, I would find a way.

I climbed halfway on him and rested my forearms, one light, one heavy and purple, on his chest and held my head up so I could look at him. I resisted the urge to blush and turn away. That look he gave me, with his eyes seeing through every façade I'd built over the years and loving me anyway, stole my breath. I halted under his gaze, swallowed, and wondered if I could ever give him the same intensity, if I could ever make his blood hot and his thoughts freeze like he did to me.

"I never said thank you. For finding the frat boy. And finding me under the arena. For everything."

"You're welcome."

"I'm sorry I pushed you away. I mean, one day we're best friends and the next I'm telling you to get out forever. I really was awful."

"You weren't awful."

I gave him a look.

"Okay, maybe you were awful. But I got it, you know. I understood. There was a lot for you to deal with. I just hated watching you hide everything, changing. I wish you'd have let me in. I knew you needed someone."

"It was easier my way. Pretending it all didn't happen. Just cut off everything that was linked to Simon and my mom and stepmom. And that included you." I felt warm tears fill my eyes and I didn't brush them away. "You, who was there with me the moment Simon was taken from me." I pictured my brother, before the chemo, when he had the most angelic mop of golden curls atop his head. I couldn't speak anymore. The tears choked me up. Josh pulled me down to him and hugged me. The way I should have let him a long time ago.

"I'm sorry I hurt you so much. I don't want to ever make you hurt like that again. I just held onto your words for so long—how you said everything would be okay but it never was after that and I blamed you for saying that and it not coming true even though I *knew* what you meant and then . . . I felt guilty blaming you. And guilty for making you hurt."

"I always hoped things would get better for you."

"Even when I told you I hated you?"

"I shouldn't have made it seem like it would be so easy. But it broke me to see you suffer after Simon died. And then your mom left."

"We were fifteen! What else could you have said? What did we know?"

"I knew I was in love with you," he said, matter-of-fact.

I touched my finger to his lips.

"I knew I loved you, too. That's why I believed everything you said to me. How could you lie to me?"

"I'm so sorry."

"You don't need to be. You didn't lie, it just took a little longer than I thought it would to become the truth."

He threaded my hair between his fingers and kissed me. "It will be okay."

"I believe you," I said against his mouth as my hand trailed across his shoulders, his chest. As my lips followed my hand. As I climbed fully atop of him and let him inside my heart and my body.

21

Charlie came with me to be my moral support as I searched for the perfect dress for graduation. I'd have liked to have bought the black dress from the fashion show—the one that led us to fundraising victory in the Spring Carnival—but it was tainted with bad memories.

So, something else. Unsurprisingly, Charlie had an amazing eye, knowing what I would look great in, after which he rushed me over to the shoe department.

"You have such great style," I said as he slipped me into the strappy sky blue heels he'd picked out.

"I know." He pulled off the strappy and traded it for an adorable silver kitten heel with a little bow in front. He helped me to my feet and looked me up and down.

"How does that feel?"

I rolled my eyes. "Does it matter? How do they look?"

"Perfect," he smiled. "I went shopping with Chelsea before she died, you know. She picked out a dress for the party after the fashion show. She knew you ladies would raise the most money."

"Of course we would have. We always did." I felt a stab of sorrow. Me and Chelsea. We could always take on the world.

"We hadn't planned on looking for one, we were just hanging out one weekend and there it was, this scarlet stunner hanging on the end aisle. We lunged for it at the same time and nearly knocked over a mannequin. The saleslady was not amused. It was short and flirty and exactly Chelsea. She tried it on and I bought it for her, as a present. It was very spur of the moment."

"That sounds like Chelsea." I smiled. "The best things in her life were never planned."

"Like you," Charlie smiled back.

#

There were parties after the graduation ceremony. Loads of them. And, had I wanted to, I could have washed the tears and mascara off my face—the fallout from all the sad goodbyes to my Delta Gamma sisters—and gone. But I didn't have anything left to prove to anyone, anywhere I needed to be other than where I wanted to be. With the person I wanted to be with, most.

As I headed home, I thought about Chelsea and her red dress that would never get worn and about people who worked so hard to look perfect. I thought about Damon and all the charges that had been brought against him and his life, ruined. I hated him for what he did to Chelsea and even to me. And yet, there was a little part of me that felt sorry for him, remembered when he'd treated me well, remembered that we had been friends of a sort. But the biggest part of me? It only wished none of it had happened in the first place.

On the Sunday after the fashion show, while I was still on a pretty high dosage of pain meds, Charlie and Josh had come by to tell me how it was they'd found me. When Charlie showed up at his house to confront him, instead of calling the police like he said he was going to, Professor Griffin confessed to the affair, but not to the murder. While he was there, Olga called and told Griffin I was distraught and that they needed to explain things to me—that she'd known about the baby, that she was planning on helping, if Chelsea would have let her.

They called my phone and when I didn't answer they called Josh, then rushed to the arena after Josh told them about my call to him. And Josh and Charlie and Professor Griffin scoured the "under", getting lost in the dark tunnels and rooms and hallways that branched off into seemingly nothing until they heard my screams and came rushing.

Just in time.

I absently fingered the scar on the inside of my shoulder blade. It would get smaller in time, the doctors had said. The detective said the same thing, when she came. Red. She came to make sure I was okay and to get a statement, to assure me none of it was my fault, that sometimes it was an unlikely person, that sometimes trusting gut feelings was the best thing to do and she was proud of me for following my instincts. The woman was a hard-ass, but if I had died after all, she'd be the one I'd have wanted on my case.

I thought about the janitor, released weeks ago, and hoped he'd made it home to visit family. I thought about Carolina, who'd covered for me so that the DG ladies didn't freak out, so that the fashion show could still go on. Who said I needed to trust fate more often.

So I was.

I leaned my head against Josh's shoulder and looked up at him.

"This is it," I said, sliding my arms around his waist. I loved his warmth and snuggles. I kissed his mouth, his chin, his neck, so smooth and good and right.

"Into the big, bad world." Josh laughed and nibbled on my ear. I thought about fighting down the thrills that were bolting up and down my body, but that was the old Katie, so instead I closed my eyes and luxuriated in the sensations.

Josh had met me at my house and now we were standing in my backyard. Appropriate, because this is where our lives had started. This was where we were launching off from, now. Dad came outside with an envelope in his hand. He stopped in his tracks and looked at me in that proud way only fathers can. He folded his hands behind his back and smiled.

"I feel like I looked away, just for a second, and in that time you went from a baby in a stroller to the most beautiful woman I've ever seen."

I swallowed, a big, full swallow, even though it hurt, and thanked the make-up gods, once again, for waterproof mascara.

"I love you, Dad," I croaked, putting bullfrogs to shame.

He came over and hugged me.

"I have something for you. For both of you. But first . . ." My father swept his eyes over Josh and then let them rest back on me. "You sure you want to be with this one? I've seen him eat dirt."

"When I was two!" Josh protested.

I grinned at them both. "Yup, he's the one."

Josh fairly beamed as my father nodded at me. "All right then. Here. And congratulations, Katie."

I opened the envelope to find a travel itinerary for me and Josh.

"Italy and Croatia. A whole month." A surprised smile burst across my face. "Thank you, Dad."

I threw my arms around him. Over his shoulder, Harriet, one of the dogs from the shelter, barked her approval. I had to adopt her, knowing Dad would be alone after I left for Stanford.

"You're welcome. I love you." He headed back to the house and I passed the itinerary to Josh to read. He tucked it away, for now.

"By the way," he said, moving close to me and resting his forehead on mine. "I didn't tell you yet how amazing you looked today. You took my breath away."

How could I not just completely fall in love with him? I mean, really. It was impossible.

"Thanks," I said. "I like your tie."

"I'd like it better if you took it off me." He wiggled his eyebrows.

"My dad might be watching," I said. But I reached for his tie anyways. I didn't have to take it off him now. There would be plenty of time for that this summer. And the months after, as we built our lives, and love, in the real world.

I stood on my tiptoes and pressed my nose against his. His eyes crinkled as he smiled at me. I loved those velvet eyes. It made me giddy whenever I discovered he had been looking at me without me noticing. Giddiness happened a lot lately.

We shared a smile, a sweet one that blended our histories and brought them to today, to tomorrow.

"Congratulations, graduate," he said.

"Dad already said that," I replied.

"I love you."

"Dad already said that, too," I grinned.

Josh leaned down and whispered something in my ear, something that made my legs weak and my chest hot. Then he took my face in his hands and covered my lips with his, leaving me with a long, lingering kiss that I felt from my toes to the top of my head.

And the thing Josh whispered in my ear?

Nobody had said that to me before.

The End.

Acknowledgements

My deepest gratitude to the many people whose talents helped this book come to be. In particular, thank you to my patient and hard-working agent, Suzie Townsend, who never lost faith in this book. And to everyone at New Leaf Literary, especially Kathleen Ortiz, Danielle Barthel, Jaida Temperly, and Jess Dallow for their wonderful insight and much-appreciated hard work on this book's behalf. Thank you also to my beta readers, idea bounce-offers and folks-who-challenge-my-process, most notably the YA Highway ladies. Finally, thank you to Paul and my pixies. For everything.

About the Author

When she was little, Kristin Halbrook wanted to be a writer, the President of the USA or the first female NFL quarterback. The first one stuck. Even when pursuing other dreams, she always took time to write, including stories for adults, teens, and children. She is the author of *Nobody But Us* (HarperTeen, 2013) and the forthcoming *Every Last Promise* (HarperTeen, April 2015). *Surfacing* is her new adult debut.

When she's not writing or reading, she's spending time with three pixies, her Mad Scot soulmate, and one grumpy cocker spaniel; traveling across oceans and time; cooking and baking up a storm; and watching waves crash and suns set on the beach. She currently lives, loves and explores in The Emerald City, though she occasionally makes wispy, dream-like plans to move to Paris or a Scottish castle one day (if just temporarily).

Follow her online @KristinHalbrook